Portrait *of* Ivan

Portrait *of* Ivan
PAULA FOX

Front Street

Asheville, North Carolina

Library of Congress Catalog Number: 74-93085

ISBN: 1-886910-60-x (pb)

The author gratefully acknowledges the permission of
Oxford University Press to quote six lines of poetry
by Edwin Muir from *Collected Poems* by Edwin Muir,
second edition Copyright © 1965.

For Arien Howe

Portrait *of* Ivan

I

"PEOPLE DON'T USUALLY READ ALOUD TO ME," SAID the boy, Ivan. "No one ever has."

"Never?" asked the painter.

"Not once. Unless you count a cereal box. The housekeeper read directions on a cereal box to me for a contest where you could win a lot of money. We were going to enter the contest together, and if we won, we were going to buy an island up in Maine I'd heard about. But she wanted to buy an island where it was warmer than Maine. We couldn't agree, so we decided not to try it."

"How about singing? Did anyone ever sing to you?" asked the painter.

"No, no ... unless you count Happy Birthday. My Uncle Gilbert and the housekeeper sang that to me last month on my eleventh birthday. Then my uncle had brandy, and the housekeeper and I ate the cake. Then we went out to the movies."

"If you don't want Miss Manderby to read to you, I'll send her away," said the painter.

"I don't suppose I'll mind," said Ivan. "Where would she go if you sent her away?"

"Wherever she likes," the painter answered.

"Am I to sit there?" asked Ivan, pointing to a wooden straight-backed chair that stood on a small platform in the middle of the room.

"If you'd like to," said the painter.

"Well—aren't you supposed to tell me where to sit?" asked the boy.

"Not this time," said the painter. "Later on I'll tell you where to sit."

Miss Manderby had not, as yet, spoken. Her eyes were closed and she looked asleep. The rocking chair in the corner where she sat rocked slightly, the way a chair does when someone has just gotten up from it and left the room. She had a black scarf wrapped around and around her head, and her white hair pushed out in little puffs like bits of shredded tissue paper. On her lap was a large closed book, and her small pale wrinkled fingers curled around its edges. Ivan could see the cover from where he was standing.

"That's an animal dressed up like a page boy," he said without interest. "I'm too old to hear about animals dressed as if they were people."

"We have to start now," said the painter. "Sit down somewhere, Ivan."

"Ivan!" exclaimed Miss Manderby, sitting up straight and opening her eyes wide. "How did you get such a name?"

"I'm going to sit on that little platform," said the boy as he stepped up on it. He sat down on the wooden chair.

"Now, I don't know how I'm supposed to look. When they take photographs of me, I don't have to think about it. Photographs are fast. There are pictures of me all over the house, on the walls, in boxes, in frames on tables. When it's winter, I can see how I looked in the summer. And when I'm sick, I can see how I looked when I'm well. There are lots of other pictures too, of houses and birds and worms and seashells. My father has seven cameras. And I have two. Actually, I have three, counting the new one he gave me for my birthday."

"It was rude of you not to answer my question," said Miss Manderby.

"I'm sorry," said the boy. "I was trying to figure out how to look."

"You're not to look any special way," said the painter. "Don't think about it."

"That might make me invisible, Mr. Mustazza," said Ivan.

"Call me Matt," said the painter.

"I asked how you came to be called Ivan," said Miss Manderby. "It's not a usual name."

"My mother was Russian," said the boy. "That's what they tell me. My Uncle Gilbert says that she left Russia in a sled pulled across the snow by horses. After the sled crossed the border, my mother went to Warsaw. I used to think a border was a line drawn on the ground. But you couldn't draw a line on snow, could you?"

Ivan looked questioningly at Miss Manderby, then at the painter. "No, you couldn't. Another one of my silly questions," he said. "I asked my father about that border. But he said my mother didn't tell him much about it because she was only three years old at the time and didn't remember. He said there were probably soldiers standing around. That's what makes a border. Soldiers."

The painter, who was sitting on a stool, stared at Ivan so steadily that Ivan felt a faint touch of fear, as though he were being asked a question he could never answer. When a camera looked at him, he did not have to see a face, just the top of someone's head or his jaw. The painter looked down at the large drawing pad on his lap, opened it to a blank page and then extracted a long thin piece of charcoal from a narrow box.

"At this point, you can move," he said. "In the chair, I mean. Not all over the studio. Later on you'll have to be still. That's why Miss Manderby is here. To read to you so that you can learn to sit like a pear in a dish. I hope the story will interest you so much that you will turn into a pear."

"I thought you were going to paint me," said the boy.

"I am going to paint you. But first I'm going to make some sketches. In that way I'll learn how you look. My hand will learn."

"How do I look?" asked Ivan.

"With all those photographs, I should think you'd know," said Miss Manderby.

"I know how the photographs look," Ivan said. "But I don't seem to ever really know how I look."

"What about a mirror?" asked Miss Manderby.

"Giselle says it brings bad luck to look in the mirror all the time. Giselle is the housekeeper. She's from Haiti. If we could have only agreed on the place to buy an island, we might have won the cereal box contest."

The painter drew quickly, turned a page and filled up a new one. To Ivan, the black lines looked like tree limbs.

"Who would you let on your island?" asked the painter.

"Giselle and her husband and her two children. Also Uncle Gilbert if he wanted to come." Miss Manderby stared at Ivan. He felt the question that was not asked. He knew they both wondered why he hadn't mentioned his father. In a way, he wanted them to ask him why his father was not to be included. It would be a thrilling question, something like the one the doctor asked when Ivan had a bad pain.

"Where does it hurt?" the doctor would inquire, and for a second, Ivan would forget his discomfort and feel quite good. But the painter and Miss Manderby said nothing. It was probably just as well. Ivan didn't really know the answer. He did know his father wouldn't like an island. There wouldn't be enough to do for someone like his father, who was always taking airplanes from one place to another or answering long-distance phone calls. Only this morning, his father had said he'd have to go to Caracas soon. Ivan knew Caracas was thousands of miles away, yet his father had sounded a little bored as though he were speaking of going to the corner store for a newspaper.

For a long time no one spoke. The room smelled of dust and other things, perhaps of the tubes of paint Ivan saw on a table, or of the thick-looking yellow liquid in the large uncapped bottle on the floor near the platform, or of all the heaps of rags on which, he guessed, brushes had been wiped because they were spotted with so many colors. Specks of dust floated in the sunlight that came through the large window. There were no rugs on the floor. In one corner of the room Ivan noticed a small, fourlegged stove standing on a table. A blue dented coffeepot sat on one of the stove's two burners. Next to it was a big white sink standing on one lopsided thick leg, behind which a number of thin silver pipes wound around each other like a metal doodle.

"I don't see how they could get a lot of people on a sled," Ivan said suddenly. "I've thought a lot about that. Besides my mother, there was her mother and her brother. Giselle doesn't know either because it never snows in Haiti."

"You're thinking of an ordinary sled," said Miss

Manderby. "I would guess it was really a sledge. A sledge would be large enough to carry people for a long distance in the winter."

"I'll draw one for you," said the painter. "Remind me later in case I forget."

"Do you like school?" asked Miss Manderby.

The boy was going to say yes, a boring answer to a boring question. Then he thought about it. "Sometimes," he said at last.

What Ivan hated was the hour he had to spend three days a week with the woman who was trying to teach him to read faster. What he liked was art class, and the library period when he could look at the little drawings in the big dictionary, things like an incandescent lamp, a hookah, a fret saw, the endocarp of a peach, the colored plates of coins, medals and the uniforms of soldiers from different historical periods. There were also books of photographs of hydroelectric dams, diesel engines, cobras, skiers jumping, monkeys.

"I didn't like it," Miss Manderby was saying in a dreamy voice. "I felt stupid all the time. Years of feeling stupid ... I never understood what people were saying to me, what they wanted me to do. All I ever wanted to do was to read. I read through all my classes. When the teacher discovered the book in my lap—and it was never the book I was supposed to have on my desk—she'd send me to the principal's office. The next day I'd do it again. They must have finally given up on me though, because during my last year of high school I managed to begin and finish every novel that Dostoevsky wrote that had been translated into English."

"Wow!" said the painter.

"Every Tuesday I went to the public library," Miss Manderby continued. "And one afternoon I was carrying so many heavy books that when I got home and my mother opened the door, I fell right down on the floor. I remember how my mother laughed and said I was hopeless."

"What's in that bottle?" asked Ivan.

"Linseed oil," said the painter.

"But then," Miss Manderby continued, as though there had been no interruption, "when my mother's eyes began to go—cataracts, you know—I began to read to her to pass the long hours. I read to her for the rest of her life. So, in the end, she was very glad that I loved to read because during the last part of her life she heard about things she hadn't dreamed existed."

"My mother isn't alive," said Ivan.

"I know," said the painter. "When your father came to see me to commission your portrait, he told me that."

"I don't remember her at all," said Ivan. Then he waited for the painter and the old lady to say something, to look at him in a certain way. But the painter continued sketching, and the old lady rocked back and forth and stared out the window.

People usually said something to him, or muttered something, or else they kissed him or touched his hair. Whatever had happened to his mother had happened a long time ago, before he was even a year old. Yet even his teachers got a certain expression on their faces when they spoke to him, especially if he hadn't done what he was supposed to do or had forgotten his homework or lost a notebook or a textbook. That special expression made him feel he was being forgiven.

But the painter and Miss Manderby did not look at him in a special way. Ivan felt cranky, and tired of sitting on the hard chair. His bottom was beginning to ache. He stood up and stretched. The painter looked up at him and nodded as though it was all right with him if Ivan had had enough of sitting. Then he turned to Miss Manderby.

"What you say about reading is interesting to me because I hardly ever read a book. Books made me restless."

"My dreams all begin with the cover of a book being opened," she said.

"Let's have a cup of coffee," said the painter, putting down the drawing pad and walking over to the stove. While he was filling the dented blue coffeepot with water, Ivan jumped off the platform and walked over to a large wooden easel he had not noticed earlier. The wood was spotted with paint, and like everything else in the studio, it looked old and used and shabby. Except for the painter, Ivan thought, who looked quite young and new for an adult.

The wooden pieces of the easel felt warm, like tree trunks in the summer. By ducking, Ivan stuck his head between the back strut that supported the easel and the crosspiece upon which the canvas would rest. He looked out at the room as though he were a picture himself.

"Here is what I look like," he said.

Miss Manderby and the painter looked at him, and the painter laughed.

"Exactly," said the painter.

"What a strange idea," observed Miss Manderby.

"Imagine a gallery full of real people looking out from frames!"

The painter dropped handfuls of coffee into the boiling water until it erupted like a small volcano. Then he snatched the pot off the burner, holding it with a paint-stained rag.

"Will you have some, Ivan?" he asked.

"Yes," said Ivan. "That's the way Giselle makes it in the morning. Before I go to school, she and I have a cup together. She's teaching me a little French. Café au lait."

"I don't have milk," said the painter. "So you'll have to drink it black."

The three of them sat near the sunny window and drank the coffee from tin mugs that burned their fingers. Ivan found the coffee bitter and strong, but he decided he would drink it black from now on. It made him feel slightly dizzy, but tough, ready for anything.

"Shall I go back and sit in the chair?" he asked when they'd finished. Miss Manderby was turning the pages of the book in her lap. "My grandfather looked like the frog footman," she said.

"That's enough for today," the painter said. "I'll draw that sledge for you before you go." He picked up the mugs and dropped them with a bang into the sink. Then he took a large sheet of paper from the table, and as Ivan came to stand beside him he began to draw a sledge with a black crayon.

"Oh!" exclaimed Ivan. "So that's how it looked!"

"Here. I'll put in a pine tree. Next Saturday when you come I'll do the horses."

Ivan looked down at the sledge. How powerful it looked! Too heavy for one horse to pull. The pine tree seemed to shrink away from it. The painter had made tracks appear so that the sledge seemed not to be stopped in the middle of a page of drawing paper, but to be on its way across the snow.

"Thanks," said Ivan, staring at the sledge. "I had no idea it would look like that."

"What are you going to do this afternoon?" asked Miss Manderby.

"Go to the movies," Ivan answered. "Giselle and I will meet her two children, Louis and Annette. Then we'll go to the movie right near where I live." The four of them would sit there in the dark that smelled of old rugs, and they would eat candy. Sometimes he and Giselle would have a whispered conversation about how silly the movie was, or how frightening.

"It's science fiction today," Ivan said. "My favorite kind."

"Mine too," said the painter. "The only kind I really like, in fact."

"I don't like science fiction at all," said Miss Manderby.

Ivan took down his jacket from the nail on the wall where the painter had hung it. He stood at the door of the big room, hesitating. In a way he didn't want to leave.

Miss Manderby was tucking bits of hair under her scarf. The painter was looking over the sketches he had made of Ivan. Between this door and Ivan's own kitchen where Giselle would be waiting for him, there were the stairs to the street, the block to the bus stop, the bus ride, the walk along the avenue to his house. Suddenly Ivan ran back into the studio, up to the bottle of linseed oil on the floor. He picked it up and sniffed at it.

"I just wanted to see what it smelled like," he said, feeling a little foolish.

"Wait!" said the painter. He dug around in a pail among some cans and tubes and bottles, and eventually produced a small plastic vial. He poured a small amount of linseed oil into it. Then he held the vial out to Ivan.

"Take it," he said. "This will remind you of the

studio until you come next week."

Going down the narrow flight of stairs, Ivan took an occasional sniff of the linseed oil, and even on the bus, when he was sure no one was watching him, he held the little bottle up to his nose. In this fashion he got all the way home, and it was almost as if he hadn't left the studio at all.

II

"Hello, Ivan," said the painter. "You're right on time."

"Hello, Mr. Mustazza."

"Call me Matt."

Miss Manderby was sitting in the rocking chair as she had been last Saturday, and if she hadn't been wearing a purple scarf instead of a black one, Ivan would have thought she had not moved for seven days. The same book was on her lap, only now it lay wide open, and from her intent downward gaze Ivan realized she was reading.

The sky was gray today. The light that came through the window was flat and lifeless, yet it made objects in the painter's studio stand out clearly so that Ivan saw some things he had not noticed the Saturday before.

"What is that?" he asked, pointing to a wooden

structure composed of a number of narrow compartments. It looked rather like a puzzle. In some of the
compartments large canvases stood on their sides.
"And where does that door go?"

"Good-day, Ivan," said Miss Manderby, looking
up from her book.

"Hello, Miss Manderby," Ivan said. She smiled
sweetly at him, but he had the feeling she wasn't too
interested in his being there. Perhaps she read to many
boys.

"That's where I keep my paintings," said Matt.
"My other paintings are in my gallery. And the little
door goes to a bathroom."

"Your gallery?" asked Ivan.

"A gallery," said Matt. "My gallery. That's where I
show my paintings from time to time. If people want
to buy them, they go to the gallery and see them
there."

"If you wrote a book," Miss Manderby said, "you
would take it to a publisher, and if the publisher liked
it, he would publish it, and then people could buy it.
That is what a gallery is like for a painter."

Ivan hung his jacket over the nail on the wall. He
saw the painter's crayon drawing of the sledge lying
on the table.

PAULA FOX

"In all those pictures in my house, there isn't one of my mother," he said. "I've looked everywhere. I even asked my Uncle Gilbert, but he said he didn't know of any. Maybe they were lost by mistake—maybe someone put them in a box and they were thrown out."

As Ivan stepped up on the platform and sat down on the wooden chair, he thought about the conversation he had had with his uncle.

Uncle Gilbert, who usually made jokes and always brought Ivan strange little gifts, such as a one dollar bill folded up and stuck inside a potato all wrapped up in yards of tissue paper, hadn't made a joke when Ivan asked him about pictures.

"I don't know what my brother did with them," he had said.

What Ivan had not told the painter was that he had looked for pictures of his mother many times before. Once he and Giselle had gone through every closet in the house, but had found nothing at all.

"Why not ask your father?" asked Miss Manderby.

"She had black hair," said Ivan, rushing by Miss Manderby's question as though he were on a bicycle. He didn't know why he hadn't asked his father.

"Today, you will have to sit quite still," said the

painter. "I want to see how the light falls on you and the chair, and I'm going to move things around a bit."

The painter didn't walk sedately to the platform where the chair was, but sprang to it in two large hops. Then he leaped on the platform, picked up the chair like a strongman, flourished it and set it down.

"Well done!" cried Miss Manderby. Ivan laughed. The chair seemed to be in the exact position it had been in before.

"Take a seat, Ivan," said the painter.

At the precise moment Ivan sat down, Miss Manderby began to read aloud, and despite the fact that Ivan did not especially want to listen, he could not help hearing what she was reading. But instead of having the effect of making him sit quietly, he found he was fidgeting more and more. He wanted to argue with the story Miss Manderby was unfolding in her thin high voice.

As if anyone, thought Ivan disgustedly, could slide through a mirror and come out the other side!

"You'd break your skull if you crawled through a mirror," he cried suddenly, interrupting Miss Manderby in the middle of a sentence.

"But it's a fairy tale," Miss Manderby protested mildly.

Ivan knew that.

"Like a dream …" said the painter.

"I don't dream," Ivan said.

"Not even when you're awake?" asked Miss Manderby.

"I like stories about things that really happened," said Ivan. "Giselle tells me about the village she used to live in up in the mountains of Haiti. Sometimes the soldiers came there from the capital, and everyone had to hide in the graveyard. My Uncle Gilbert has stories about the war. Once he won a camel race in Cairo."

"I suppose my whole life has been a dream," said Miss Manderby reflectively. She reached up and tucked in a bit of ruffled hair under the scarf.

"What about the sledge?" the painter asked Ivan. "Isn't that a kind of dream?"

"That really happened," replied Ivan, feeling stubborn, feeling warm and stuffy as though he'd gotten stuck in last year's sweater.

"But we can only guess what really happened," said the painter insistently, looking straight at Ivan. "No one was there to take a photograph. You heard about it from your uncle who heard about it from someone else. You told me. Miss Manderby told us about the sledge. Today I'll draw the horses that pulled the sledge. But I don't really know how many there were, or what kind they were."

"And you like science fiction," said Miss Manderby.

"That's science," Ivan said.

"If you ask me," grumbled Miss Manderby, "science is the biggest fiction of all!"

"It's time to have our coffee," said the painter. He got up and went to his stove, singing to himself in a loud voice in what Ivan thought was a foreign language. Then he realized the painter was just making up words.

"Coffeiolla ..." sang the painter. Ivan couldn't help laughing.

"What movie will you see today?" Miss Manderby asked Ivan while they were drinking the coffee.

"I can't go today," said Ivan. "Giselle is taking Louis to the dentist this afternoon."

"Oh, then what will you do instead?" she asked.

"I'm making a collection of photographs of radio circuit paths," replied Ivan. "Actually, I've only found one picture so far. But I have a lot of magazines my uncle brought to look through."

"What on earth is a circuit path?" asked Miss Manderby.

"It's the path over which the electric current flows," said Ivan, pleased to give her some information for a change.

"Next you'll be telling me that electricity isn't a fairy tale!" she said.

"Maybe you'd like to come with me to an opening," said the painter to Ivan. "A friend of mine is showing some metal sculptures this afternoon right near here." Without waiting for Ivan's answer, he went over to his junk table. When he returned he was holding a small plastic rectangle which he placed on Ivan's knee. One side of the rectangle showed an intricate arrangement of silver lines imbedded in the plastic. Ivan turned it over. Attached by staples to the back were nine small brown tubes, each circled by two orange lines, and below them were ten tiny crystal tubes.

"That's an old radio circuit," said the painter. "I bought it for ten cents in a junk shop."

"A real one!" exclaimed Ivan.

"Real!" cried Miss Manderby. "Why, it looks like pure magic to me!"

"You can have it," said the painter to Ivan. "How about it? You want to go to that opening?"

"Yes," said Ivan. "I'll have to call Giselle."

"There's the phone," said the painter. "Underneath

those rags. You come too, Miss Manderby."

"I have to go home and feed my little cat," said Miss Manderby.

"Bring him along," said the painter.

After Ivan had telephoned Giselle and told her he was going to an opening with the painter, and she had said all right, she'd leave his supper in the oven, he stopped to look at the crayon drawing of the sledge. The painter came to stand next to him.

"We'll make it four horses," he said.

"You could make it three," said Miss Manderby. "Then it would be a troika. I learned that from reading."

Ivan wondered if she were reproaching him. Someday, perhaps, he would be able to read faster, although he doubted he would ever want to read the kind of books Miss Manderby read.

The painter was drawing quickly. As Ivan watched, he saw the horses emerge almost as though they were breaking right through the white paper, springing from the spot they had always been to place themselves so perfectly between the traces, straining forward now as they pulled the empty massive sledge.

It seemed to Ivan, although it couldn't be true, that more snow had fallen on the branches of the little pine tree since he had looked at it a week ago. He wanted to touch that tree, and without realizing it, his hand went out toward it. The painter stopped drawing and looked at Ivan's outstretched hand. "Go ahead," he said.

Ivan ran his fingers across the tree and felt the waxy smoothness of the crayon strokes. Then he took his hand away. Yet it was a tree with snow on its thick boughs!

"Pretty good, eh?" asked the painter, smiling.

Miss Manderby had joined them and was peering down at the drawing. "You'll want to pile up some fur rugs on the sledge," she said. "Although that could wait until you get the people in it. And a sentry box would show it was a border."

"Next Saturday," said the painter. "It's time to go to Harry's opening."

A block from Matt's studio, they parted from Miss Manderby.

"Perhaps I'll join you later," she said, after she shook hands with them both.

"She'll probably forget once she's in her room," said the painter to Ivan as they walked on down the street. "She'll get started on some book and forget what day it is. But then, she might not. If she feels lonely, she'll come along."

Ivan was startled. It was unusual to hear one adult speaking of another in such a way. He thought about Miss Manderby and how old she was. It was unsettling to think about someone so old being lonely. But it pleased him that the painter had talked to him about it.

"Here we are," said Matt. He had come to a halt in front of what appeared to be a small store. But the glass window, instead of being filled with canned fruit or shoes or tennis rackets, was filled with people. They were gathered around a little machine that was tossing ping-pong balls at itself with a small metal arm. As the ping-pong balls described half-circles in the air, all the people laughed.

Matt took Ivan's hand and led him down two steps and into the store, which was packed with people.

"Kinetic!" shouted someone over Ivan's head.

"Look around," said Matt. "But don't try to see Harry's work. You can never see an artist's work at an opening, just the people."

At that moment a large soft-looking man with an enormous beard caught Matt by the arm. "Here's the sculptor himself," said Matt, grinning. "This is Ivan, Harry. He's never been to an opening."

"I wish I'd never been to an opening," said Harry

in a glum voice. "Listen to that noise! Look at all those elbows! Nobody would notice if I left. Nobody would even notice if I got up on the ceiling. They've drunk all my wine punch. But I might have a little ginger ale left. Ivan, you want some ginger ale? Come with me. We'll fight our way through to that table over there."

He grabbed Ivan's arm and said, "Push. Don't look!" But a thin tall lady wearing a brown blanket around her shoulders and earrings that touched the blanket, flung her arms around Harry's neck.

"Fabulous!" she shouted. "The work is gorgeous!"

Ivan happened to look down at the floor and saw that Harry was wearing bedroom slippers, and one of his socks was either on inside out or didn't match the other. The lady in the blanket was wearing a wide orange ribbon around one of her ankles. Harry let go of Ivan's arm and a group of people, as though carried by a strong tide, surged between them. Ivan found himself in another part of the room. There was a little more breathing space here, and Ivan was able to spot another one of Harry's sculptures. This one was composed of two long metal arms, attached to a base, and moving slowly back and forth. Each time the two arms passed each other they seemed to hesitate slightly.

For some reason that little pause made Ivan laugh. "That's right, my boy!" cried a voice from somewhere.

"He shouldn't laugh," said another voice sternly. "It's a serious work."

"It's my work, and I say he should laugh!" said the first voice crossly. A paper cup full of ginger ale was pressed into Ivan's hand. Looking up, he saw Harry once more. "Grab it before they carry me off!" cried the sculptor.

It was warm ginger ale, but Ivan was glad the sculptor had remembered him, and he drank it all down. When he looked up, Harry had disappeared. His place was now filled by two thin men who were talking to each other. It was evident to Ivan that neither one was listening to the other, yet every now and then they both paused, exactly like Harry's sculpture of the two metal arms, then started talking again.

Around them were more people, and around those people were still others, and around those others were Harry's machines, circling and throwing ping-pong balls, small metal hammers striking metal bars, and metal balls tumbling down metal ramps. The floor was disappearing under the paper cups and paper napkins that were being dropped, somewhat sneakily, Ivan observed, from people's hands. Tobacco smoke was rising from pipes and cigars and cigarettes, and the level of the noise had risen so much that Ivan could not hear separate voices anymore.

Except when school was dismissed directly from the auditorium, or when he had been caught in a bus during the rush hours, or in gym when several classes played together, Ivan had not ever been buried in such a crowd of people. The house was always so quiet—he and Giselle didn't even have to raise their voices when they talked to each other from different rooms—and Uncle Gilbert spoke almost in a whisper, although he did have a loud laugh. And Ivan's father said things in a low voice in such short clear sentences that Ivan could almost see the punctuation. Especially the periods. Bang! End of sentence. Ivan kept his own radio low in the evenings because when his father was home and noticed that Ivan had homework to do, he made him turn it off. Television was mostly so boring that Ivan didn't care whether the sound was on or not. But what was happening to him in this room was that he felt he was drowning in a laundry bag.

He dove through the crowd with his head down,

and plowed his way to the door and outside. When he looked back at the window, he had the impression the old store was going to burst at its seams and all the people come flying out in straight lines like the man he and Uncle Gilbert had once seen at the circus—the man who had been shot out of a cannon.

He noticed the ping-pong ball machine had stopped throwing ping-pong balls at itself, possibly because three people were leaning against it. A squashed paper cup covered the metal arm. At the very center of the crowd inside the store, Ivan saw Harry whose head appeared, then disappeared as though he were jumping up and down on a small trampoline. All at once, as Harry's head bobbed up, Ivan saw a hand rise up out of the crowd and pluck his beard right off his face. Harry descended instantly and did not appear again until he and Matt burst through the door and out onto the sidewalk.

"Wow!" said Harry. Ivan stared at the beard that Harry was carrying in his hand. "Here. Take it, kid!" said Harry. "I've got eleven more at home." And he thrust the beard at Ivan, who discovered it was made of dozens of little scraps of brown paper, as curly as Christmas ribbon, glued to a piece of rough cloth. Matt was smiling at him.

"How did you like the opening?" he asked.

"No one was looking at anything," said Ivan.

"That's the way it always is," said Harry. "But the ones who really want to see my work will come back."

The opening had reminded Ivan of a birthday party he had gone to when he was very little. In the first place, he'd gotten sick to his stomach even before they got there, and Giselle had made him sit down right on the sidewalk and bend his head until the dizziness went away. In the second place, he'd been so excited when he got to the house where the birthday party was that he forgot the boy's name. And when Giselle came back to get him at five o'clock, it was as if he hadn't even been to a birthday party. He thought of telling Matt about it, but he decided Harry wouldn't be much interested. Harry was looking back nervously at the store.

"I'll have to go back in," he said. "But I'll meet you at Luigi's later." Then he turned to Ivan and said, "Thanks for coming to my opening."

"Can you have supper with us?" Matt asked Ivan. "You like Italian food?"

"Spaghetti?" asked Ivan.

"There's more to it than that. Can you?"

"Yes, I can," said Ivan. Actually, he didn't know if

he could. But there was no one to ask at the moment except himself, and he said yes.

"See you later," said Harry. "I'm going into that room backwards."

Matt and Ivan walked for a few blocks, then Matt said, "Here's Luigi's."

Inside Luigi's there was sawdust on the floor and a delicious smell in the air. Hanging over the shelves of wine bottles was a dark shadowed photograph of a lady, and standing beneath the picture was an old, old woman who smiled at Ivan. Her white hair was twisted in a knot, her nose was very long and she looked vaguely like the lady in the picture. "That's the padrona herself," said Matt.

"Come sta, Matt?" she said to the painter.

"Béne," replied Matt. "Here, I brought a friend along."

"Very nice," said the old lady, looking at Ivan.

A very old waiter took them to a big round table covered with a white cloth on which there was a straw basket of bread and a bowl full of grated cheese. Matt handed Ivan a menu, and Ivan handed it right back.

"I don't think I could even read it in English," he said.

"I'm going to get you fettucine," said Matt.

The old waiter sighed as he brought them their food, and sighed as he mixed a salad for them right there on the table. "I'm getting old," he said. "Even olive oil has become too heavy."

The fettucine, a thin noodle with cream and butter, was delicious. Matt had a glass of red wine and a soup bowl full of steely blue shells.

"Put down Harry's beard," he said. "It'll get in the fettucine." Ivan noticed that he was still clutching the beard, which had stuck slightly to his wrist.

"What's that you're eating?" he asked.

"Mussels," said Matt. "Edible mollusks. Have one?"

"I'd rather not," said Ivan.

"How's yours?"

"Good!" said Ivan.

"Eat everything," said the old waiter as he passed their table carrying a tray full of food for some other people.

After a while Harry arrived, along with the lady in the brown blanket and several other people who all sat down at Matt's table. Soon the table was loaded with platters of food—some dishes that Ivan hadn't known existed, such as squid which Harry explained was a kind of octopus. Everyone ate from the platters and tore the long loaf of white bread with his fingers and stuffed the large soft pieces of bread into his mouth. Everyone talked and laughed at the same time, but it was not as bad as the opening since occasionally someone really listened to someone else.

What was best from Ivan's viewpoint was that no one seemed to feel obligated to ask him questions. "Try this scallopine," someone would suggest, giving him a forkful of veal. "Do have some of my broccoli," someone else would say. It was like being part of everything while remaining invisible.

For dessert Matt ordered a small paper cup full of ice cream for Ivan. "Biscuit tortoni," he said. "Very special." And it was. Then Ivan had a cup of coffee, very black and dense, into which Matt twisted a small piece of lemon peel. When Ivan looked up from watching the lemon peel sink into the coffee, he saw Miss Manderby standing behind Matt. Harry got her a chair from an empty table nearby and everyone moved over to make room for her. No one seemed surprised to see her, and all she said was, "I hoped I'd find you here."

"Well," said Harry, "it was a good opening. But this is the best part."

"Fabulous!" said the lady in the brown blanket,

41

mopping up the sauce in her plate with a piece of bread.

Matt took Ivan home on the bus and told him about the lady in the blanket who spent every summer out in the desert in New Mexico, teaching Navajo children how to read, about Harry who had to teach art in a school so that he could have a few days free for himself to work on his metal sculptures, and about the other two painters who had eaten with them. One went to Italy whenever he could because he loved that country and it was cheaper to live there, and so he worked in a big department store all winter long to earn enough money to pay for his fare to Milan. And the other worked in a motorcycle shop half the year so that he could go to Vermont in the summer and autumn where he had a big barn in which to paint.

"Don't they get enough money for their paintings so they don't have to do all those other things?" asked Ivan.

Matt said, "No, not enough unless they are famous. But they don't complain because they are doing the work they want to do."

Ivan thought for a moment, then asked, "Is that why you do portraits of people? So you can have money to do other painting?"

Matt didn't answer right away but looked out the bus window. Ivan could see his reflection in the glass.

"Yes," he said at last. "But I like doing portraits too. Not always, but sometimes. I like doing yours."

Ivan thought about the painters, all doing work they liked to do. He wondered about Uncle Gilbert and Giselle and his father. Did they like their work?

When they got to Ivan's house, Matt said, "Don't forget your beard."

"Thanks," said Ivan, picking up the beard, which had stuck to the bus seat.

"See you next week," said Matt.

"Thanks for the fettucine, too," said Ivan. Ivan took his key out of his pocket and opened the door. The hall light was on. He stood there for a moment, listening. Then he looked into the mirror over the hall table where the mail was always left. He held the beard up to his face and patted it down until what was left of the glue adhered to his cheeks. He looked very strange.

He tiptoed down the hall, past his father's room. He could see the numbers on his father's clock shining from the night table. Suddenly his father shot up from the bed.

"Who ..." he stammered. Then his father ran to the door.

"Good heavens, Ivan! What's that? A beard?"

"A paper beard," replied Ivan.

Surprisingly, his father began to laugh.

"I thought I'd slept for twenty years, and you'd grown up to be a little old man with a beard!" His father was laughing so hard now that he leaned up against the door frame.

"Listen!" he said. "I want to take a picture of you in that beard. Wait a minute!"

"Couldn't you just remember it?" asked Ivan, feeling very sleepy.

Ivan told Giselle about the opening, Harry, the woman in the brown blanket, and the painters. Then he asked her, "Do you like your work?"

Giselle put down the frying pan she was scouring and repeated, "Like my work?" Then she laughed and shrugged her shoulders and said, "C'est la vie!" which, Ivan knew, meant, "That's life!"

She sat down at the kitchen table where Ivan had been doing his homework. "I wanted to have a little boutique, a shop, in Port-au-Prince. I would have designed clothes and hats. My shop would have been filled with white bird cages for parrots, and little straw chairs and flowers. All the paintings on the walls would have been by Haitian painters, and I would have sold them to the tourists. But who would have given me the money to buy the bird cages and the cloth and the pins and the thread? Who would have come to buy my clothes? And the painters are all starving now."

Giselle did not seem to be speaking to him at all, and Ivan felt sad as though a car had driven off and left him on a street corner.

"If you liked it so much, why didn't you stay in Haiti?" he asked.

"My husband could not get work there. I could not get work. We had to come here. Now my children are forgetting how to speak French."

Ivan picked up his social studies textbook and opened it to the chapter on irrigation. When he looked at all that print, he felt as if he were being bitten by an army of mosquitoes. It was a long chapter, and he should have started to study it on the weekend instead of waiting until now. He felt like crying.

"But in some ways it's not so bad here," Giselle said. She smiled. "And I like you."

The next morning she brought him a little clay rooster. "A Haitian artist made that," she said. "Now he is living in Chicago, cleaning up offices at night."

When Uncle Gilbert came to dinner on Wednesday, Ivan asked him, "Do you like your work?"

"What an odd question," remarked Uncle Gilbert.

"Now, let me see ..." He unwrapped his cigar and, as usual, handed Ivan the label. Although Ivan felt he was getting too old to wear paper rings, he slid the label on his finger.

"Yes, I do, rather," said Uncle Gilbert, after he had lit his cigar. "You never know what extraordinary coins will come jingling into the shop in someone's pocket. Some old lady who went to Egypt years ago decides to sell her third-century Egyptian bronze coins. And when I open some of the great collection catalogs and see the coins of the Greek world, I get positively dizzy. And when I place a Maria Theresa taler, dated 1780, on a tray and see it through my glass case and think of the hands that cast it, the hands that used it, I could jump for joy!"

He handed a coin to Ivan. "I brought you this," he said. "It's an 1889 silver dollar. Quite valuable." Ivan looked at the coin, which was very handsome. Uncle Gilbert said reflectively, "I wanted to be an archaeologist in my youth. In a way, I suppose I am.

"Why didn't you become an archaeologist?" asked Ivan, wondering what that was.

"We didn't have enough money in the family to pay for studies. It was during the Depression, Ivan, and we all had to go to work."

"And what did my father want to do?" asked Ivan.

Uncle Gilbert blew out a huge puff of smoke. "I don't know," he said. "I really don't know."

Ivan didn't ask the question of his father, but he considered asking his homeroom teacher, Miss Frency. It was during a study period and Miss Frency was writing the day's homework on the blackboard. Ivan observed there were chalk lines all over her dark blue suit where she had leaned against the board. He went up and stood behind her. Finally, she turned around and looked down at him. A pencil was stuck through her hair, and her glasses had chalk dust on the lenses.

"Yes?" she asked.

"Can I get a drink of water?"

"Can't you wait till the end of the period? It's only five minutes more."

"All right," he said. He couldn't figure out why he hadn't asked her. Maybe because she was so chalky.

"What's an archaeologist?" Ivan asked Miss Manderby on Saturday.

"A digger," she replied. "A person who can find and understand the past that is buried in the earth. Go look at Matt's work table over there. What if you dug that up in five hundred years and everything had been preserved? What would you be able to tell by just looking at those things?"

Ivan went to the table and looked. The more he looked, the more he saw. There were pencils of different shapes and colors, pens, reeds of bamboo. There were razor blades and knives, feathers and bits of cloth and coiled pieces of wire. There was a rusty, dried-up apple core, a dented pot, small tin cans, blobs of dried paint, pieces of wood, string, broken bits of clay, charcoal and crayons and a box of pastels, bottles of ink, boxes of lead.

"He'd be able to tell that Matthew Mustazza had been a junk man," said Matt.

Ivan picked up a gray feather. "In photographs," he said, "everything is smooth."

"Archaeologists tell how it all began," said Miss Manderby. "They can dig up a whole city that hasn't seen the light of day for four thousand years."

"Sit down, Ivan," said Matt. "Let's get started." Miss Manderby did not read from her book. Instead, she told Ivan about a buried city called Troy, and a terrible war there that had gone on for years, and how once people had thought Troy and its wars were only legends. Then a young man named Heinrich

Schliemann had gone to a place in Turkey near the Dardanelles. And there, among the ruins of the hill of Hissarlik, he had dug up not one but many cities, and one of them had been Troy.

"If you would like to have a cup of chocolate at my house after you're through here, I'll show you pictures of Troy," she said. "You too, Matt."

"I'd like that," said Ivan, more interested in seeing Miss Manderby's house than in pictures of Troy. "But I have to be home in time to meet Annette and Louis and Giselle to go to a movie.

Just before they left Matt's studio, Matt said, "We forgot the sentry box."

While Miss Manderby and Ivan watched, Matt drew a sentry box with a soldier standing inside. Then he drew another soldier, running toward the sledge, his hand outstretched as though to bring the horses to a halt. Both soldiers wore fuzzy black hats and dark capes.

"I don't think they're wearing the right uniforms," commented Miss Manderby. "When Ivan's mother crossed that border, the Czar had fallen. You've got them wearing some kind of prerevolutionary costume."

"Perhaps these sentries were so far from Moscow

they hadn't heard the news yet," said Matt. He was drawing more trees.

There was a forest now, where there had been only one pine tree, and the sledge appeared to have just emerged into the clearing where the sentries waited. Ivan thought how empty the sledge looked! It was like a ghost story, the soldier running with his hand outstretched, the rearing horses, the trees bent with snow, the empty sledge.

Miss Manderby lived a few blocks from Matt's studio in a little brownstone house. As Ivan could tell from all the mailboxes in the entryway, a number of other people lived in that house too. They climbed up four stories to the top floor, where Ivan saw a small door that looked as if it had been made just to accommodate Miss Manderby. Matt had to stoop to enter her apartment.

As soon as the door opened, a gray cat ran to their feet and looked up at them.

"Alyosha, my dear!" exclaimed Miss Manderby. "How are you?"

Miss Manderby lived in one small room in which there were two windows and a skylight in the ceiling. There were chairs and tables and a black couch without legs, and a little stove and a narrow cot. All that was uninteresting. What was different about

Miss Manderby's room, unlike any other room Ivan had ever visited, was books.

There must have been thousands of books, piled up on the floor, squeezed into bookcases, heaped up on tables, on the window sills, even in the middle of the stove between the burners. Because of the books, it was not possible to walk from one point to another in a straight line. Ivan said it was like walking through a forest, and Miss Manderby nodded.

"Well, they once were part of a forest," she said. "Think how many trees were cut down to make the paper for just this handful of books!"

Ivan didn't say so, but he thought to himself that he would have preferred to have the trees.

"Did you read them all?" he asked her.

"Yes, yes..." said Miss Manderby as she mixed cocoa and milk in a little bowl that she had set down on a pile of books. "And some I have read more than once." She put down the spoon and actually ran to one of the book shelves.

"Such as this one," she cried, taking a book and putting it on Ivan's lap. "Treasure Island," he read. "And this one!" she said, and put it on the first. It was titled The Idiot. "And this one …" and she added another. "Great Expectations," read Ivan.

She darted back and forth, between bookcases and Ivan, until she had piled up ten books on Ivan's lap. She was out of breath. "And five times five times more," she said. "Oh, the milk!" She ran to the stove and turned down the flame under a pan of milk and added the cocoa-and-milk mixture to it.

"It would take me a million years," Ivan said, almost to himself, "just to read these."

Matt lifted them off his lap and put them down on the floor.

"Miss Manderby is a witch," Matt said. "She can read a book just by looking at the cover, can't you Miss Manderby?"

"If it's written in English," said Miss Manderby gravely.

It's hard to tell when she's serious, Ivan thought. Her voice hardly ever changed, even when it was loud, but moved along like a line of print.

She brought them their cups of cocoa on a little painted tray, and a plate of crumbly cookies. Then she selected from a bookcase a large volume that she opened.

"No one believed Schliemann," she said, leaving her own cup of cocoa untouched. "But he knew that legends are part of truth." She held the book out to

Ivan. "This was published in 1876. You can tell it's an old book by taking a whiff of it. Just open it to the middle and sniff."

Ivan sniffed. The book had the smell of an attic on a rainy day. Hadn't he spent such a day at someone's house in the country? In an old attic full of dusty black trunks and piles of damp National Geographic magazines with pictures of glowing mountains and strange fish?

There were no photographs in the book, only faded brownish drawings of vases and small idols. But at the back of the book, Ivan found a map folded into three sections and he drew it out slowly as Miss Manderby leaned over him.

"The Plateau of Hissarlik," she murmured. "The Great Tower of Ilium ... the mosaic anterior to the Epoch of Priam."

"She's weaving a spell, Ivan," said the painter.

And indeed, Miss Manderby seemed in a trance herself. Then she said in a matter-of-fact voice, "Finish your cocoa before it gets cold."

It was a pleasant hour. The gray cat came and sat next to Ivan on the couch, curled up and purred. Matt and Miss Manderby spoke of Harry and the opening, and whether or not the food at Luigi's was as good this year as it had been last year. Then it was time to leave.

"You may come again and look at the book of Troy," said Miss Manderby.

"Thanks," said Ivan.

"Or anything else that strikes your fancy," she said, waving her hand at the books.

As Ivan went to meet Giselle and her children, he wondered about the book called The Idiot. For a while, in October, that had been a popular word in his class. Everyone was always calling everyone else "Idiot!" even if someone just shifted in his chair. Now fink and creep had come back into fashion.

Giselle and her children were waiting for him in front of his door. Annette waved both her hands when she saw him.

"It's going to be scary," she said. "I can tell by the name of the movie—The Lost People of Planet T."

Louis said, "I never get scared."

IV

"I HAVE A VACATION STARTING THURSDAY," SAID IVAN the following week. He had come on Friday afternoon and was carrying his school books. "So my father told me to tell you I could come any day of the week."

"I've got some news for you too," Matt said. He was standing in front of the easel upon which he had placed a canvas. Nearby was a table with tubes of paint arranged in a row and a large piece of glass and a number of paintbrushes. "My news is that I have to go away for a few weeks."

"I don't have any news," said Miss Manderby, who was, as usual, sitting in the rocking chair. "Except that I'm here."

"Where are you going?" asked Ivan, his voice very low because he felt awful, as though things were about to change for the worse.

"I'm going to Florida for a peculiar reason, replied Matt. "I am going to visit a man named Mr. Crown who lives down by a river near Jacksonville. He has sold his house to a company that is going to build a country club on his land. Now, the special thing about the Crown house is that it was once the main house of a large plantation, and when they tear it down to put up the clubhouse, and cut down all the trees to make the golf course, that will be the end of a certain kind of special Southern architecture. Mr. Crown wants me to make paintings and drawings of the house so that people will always be able to see what it once looked like."

"Why doesn't he take some photographs?" asked Ivan.

"He feels that paintings will show more of what things are really like."

"But a picture can show exactly that," said Ivan. "No, it can't," said Miss Manderby. "Because a house, because nothing, is exactly what it looks like."

Ivan shot her an impatient glance. A few weeks! What about his portrait? What about the sledge?

"When I come back," Matt was saying, "we'll go right ahead with you, Ivan."

"Is that the kind of work you do so you can afford to do the work you want?" asked Ivan.

"Not exactly," said Matt. "I'm pretty interested in this job. I've never been to Florida."

"Neither have I," said Miss Manderby.

"Neither have I," said Ivan.

"Let's begin," said Matt.

Ivan sat quietly, not because he was interested in the Mad Hatter, or all those nuts passing plates back and forth about which Miss Manderby was reading, but because he was too sad to be restless.

"You look down in the dumps," said Matt after a short time. He put down the pencil with which he had been working. Ivan wasn't even interested enough to go and look at the canvas and see what Matt had been doing.

"Time for coffee," said the painter. Ivan didn't look up.

"How would you like to go along, Ivan?" asked the painter. "How about it? You and Miss Manderby and I. Harry is going to loan me his car. He calls it a car, although nobody else might. It's about forty years old and even has vases in it for flowers."

"Could my cat go?" asked Miss Manderby.

"Why not?"

"I could pack a lovely lunch for the first day of travel," she said. "Deviled eggs and cupcakes occur to me, and I'm sure I'll think of other things."

Ivan was already dialing his father's office. "This is Ivan," he said to the switchboard operator. Then he repeated it to his father's secretary, and finally to his father himself.

"Yes, Ivan. What can I do for you?"

"Can I go to Florida with Matt and Miss Manderby?"

"Right now?"

"On Thursday, when school is over for the vacation."

Ivan's father was so quiet that Ivan thought he'd perhaps forgotten he was talking to someone on the phone and had gone off somewhere to another office. Then he heard a sound like a paper clip dropped into a dish. In fact, Ivan knew it was a paper clip. His father always carried a number of them in his jacket pocket, and when he was thinking he often dropped them into whatever receptacle was handy, as though they were unnecessary thoughts he was getting rid of.

Trying to speak in short clear sentences, Ivan explained the purpose of the trip, Matt's commission to paint the plantation house, Harry's offer of a car and Miss Manderby's promise of a picnic.

"You know quite a few people, don't you?" his father said when Ivan had finished talking. "I think it's all right for you to go. Giselle could have a vacation. Besides, I had planned to go to Caracas soon. I might just as well go a week from now as later on, and I can pick you up on my way back. How's the portrait coming?"

"I can go!" shouted Ivan to Matt.

"What?" said his father.

"I was telling everybody ..."

"Oh. Nice to talk to you, Ivan."

There was a click and Ivan put down the phone, wondering for a second if his father had gotten him mixed up with a businessman named Ivan.

Matt asked Ivan to sit a while longer. It was hard to be still now. Ivan felt as if he were actually running along a road map, downhill all the way to Florida. Even Miss Manderby seemed excited. She kept interrupting the story she was reading to ask Matt about the plantation, and if he thought they'd have books or should she bring a little collection of her own, and whether he preferred ham or cheese sandwiches.

"I can't sit still," Ivan said at last.

"Okay. Then wriggle," said Matt.

Just before Ivan left to go home, he and Miss

Manderby and Matt went to look at the drawing of the sledge.

"It's time to put someone in it," said Matt, picking up the black crayon.

"The driver?" suggested Miss Manderby.

"Right!" said Matt. He began to draw. Soon a massive tall fellow in a big fur hat stood at the front of the sledge, a whip hanging from one hand.

"That's Harry!" exclaimed Ivan.

"So it is," said Matt. "We'll put back his brown beard."

The sledge still looked empty.

"Now it needs your grandmother and your uncle and your mother," said Miss Manderby. It always surprised Ivan to hear about relatives he had never known.

"My Uncle Vladimir lives in Paris. My father says he'll take me to Paris someday to meet him. But my grandmother was very old when she arrived in France. Uncle Gilbert says she died of being tired."

"I wish I were Russian," said Miss Manderby. "Then I could read Tolstoy in his own language."

When Ivan saw his father that evening, his father said, "Going to Florida, eh?" as though Ivan had reached the decision to go all by himself.

PAULA FOX

The week passed in fits and starts. Sometimes it was as though Ivan slid down a slide right to evening. Other days, the minutes crawled and crept and even seemed to stop as though there were a hole in time.

Uncle Gilbert gave him a five dollar bill, hidden in the index finger of an old gray suede glove, which in turn had been wrapped up in a page from a Greek newspaper, which had then been stuffed into an oil-skin tobacco pouch. Giselle packed his summer shirts, last year's bathing suit and too many socks into a canvas bag.

She sighed frequently, and finally Ivan asked her if she was glad he was going away. She said, no, no, she was glad to have some time of her own though, to clean her house and have an eye examination, and buy shoes for Louis who was growing so fast she could almost see him grow, and to spend a Saturday with her husband just walking around, now that the weather was getting warmer.

He was sorry he had asked her because her answers seemed to reproach him. He had never really thought about her house, or Louis needing shoes, and what she was missing by having to spend those Saturdays with him because his father was so frequently out of town on business trips. And the truth is, he didn't think about it a great deal after she spoke to him about her own life away from him. He was too excited about the trip.

Still, now and then when he looked at her, she seemed different to him, not only the Giselle who was always there, who put his meals on the table and taught him a few words of French, but someone else, like Matt and Miss Manderby and Harry.

He told Miss Frency, his homeroom teacher, that he was going to Florida. She said: "Florida. Generally low and flat, many swamps, most extensive in south. Oranges, dairy products, cattle, tomatoes, grapefruit, tobacco, snap beans. Textiles, paper, lumber, machinery. July mean temperature, 82.1 degrees Fahrenheit. Land area is 54,252 square miles."

"Oh!" said Ivan.

"Enjoy yourself," said Miss Frency, wiping the chalk dust from her eyeglasses.

On Wednesday Ivan's father took him out to dinner to a restaurant stuffed with large red velvet furniture. There were three different size glasses at each table place.

"Have anything you like," said his father, waving his arm as if he meant Ivan had permission to take the whole restaurant home in his pocket. The menu was in French so Ivan said he'd have whatever his father had. This was a serious error, as it turned out. He managed to eat two of the snails, a few kidneys, and one bite of a soft, creeping white cheese that reminded him of the star of a science fiction movie called The Creeping Thing from Galaxy Zero.

Then his father gave him a new wallet. Inside it was money. "Give the money to Mr. Mustazza," he said. "But keep a few dollars for yourself. I have put in the wallet a list of telephone numbers, home, office, my secretary, Giselle, Uncle Gilbert, and the hotel in which I will be staying in Caracas."

Ivan suddenly felt strange, as though it was his father who was going away, not him; as though he were going to be left behind.

"Incidentally," said his father, "don't forget your camera. It's always a good idea to take a few snapshots so you know where you've been."

"Matt says to travel light," said Ivan.

"Best not to be underequipped," replied his father. "Who is this Miss Manderby, by the way?"

Miss Manderby-by-the-way, repeated Ivan to himself, and replied, "She's an old lady who reads to me."

"Ought to be quite a trip," said his father, signing his

name to the check the waiter presented. "I'll run you over to Mr. Mustazza's tomorrow after school. What time do you get out? I'll just be able to manage it."

At noon the next day, Ivan found his father waiting for him in a taxi in front of the school. Ivan's canvas bag was on the floor and his camera, which he had forgotten at the last moment, on the seat.

"You forgot the camera," said his father. "I thought the newest one would be the best to take."

In front of the building where Matt had his studio, a strange trio stood among several boxes and suitcases and an enormous picnic basket. All three of them were staring at a black car that gleamed in the sunlight. Ivan had never seen such a car except in photographs. A little silver statue of a winged lady rode its hood. It had window shades and running boards, and Ivan could see two little triangular vases on the inside of the back seat, tacked up near each door. There were flowers in the vases.

"What's that?" asked Ivan's father.

"It must be Harry's car," said Ivan.

"Well, of course it's a car. In fact, my father had one exactly like it. Never had time to polish it up though. Too busy with his patients, driving all over the countryside."

"Was he a doctor?"

"Hadn't I told you that?"

"No," said Ivan. "What about my other grand-father? My mother's father?"

"He sold rugs," said Ivan's father.

"In a store?"

"No, no . . . he was a rug merchant. Oriental rugs. He traveled all over the East, China and India and Turkey, buying and selling rugs. When your mother and grandmother and uncle had to leave Russia, they took with them several very small rugs. But they were so valuable that after they sold them in Paris they were able to live for several years on the proceeds."

"Why didn't my grandfather go with the others?"

"I don't know that part of the story," said Ivan's father. "I think everyone had to leave in a great hurry."

"Could he still be alive?"

"It's possible, but not likely," said Ivan's father. The taxi halted, and Ivan's father asked the driver to wait. Then he walked over to Matt.

Ivan ran to Miss Manderby. "There were Oriental rugs in the sledge," he said. "My grandmother took them to Paris to sell."

"We'll tell Matt about that later," she said. "Guess what I have in this box?"

Ivan noticed a large box on the sidewalk with holes punched in the top. "Alyosha," she said. "I'll let him out in the car. And guess what I have in this picnic hamper that belonged to my dear mother?"

"Cupcakes?" asked Ivan, waving at Harry, who was polishing the silver statue of the winged lady on the car hood.

"Apple strudel and brownies, deviled eggs and roast beef, potato salad and ham and chicken, raisins and carrots, apples and pears, and a thermos of coffee and one of tea, and a little supper for Alyosha in a plastic bag."

"I wish I were going with you," said Harry, walking over to join them. "What a wonderful day! What a good time you'll have! What a marvelous automobile!"

"What a picnic!" cried Miss Manderby.

"How do you do," called Ivan's father. "You must be Miss Manderby. My mother had a picnic hamper just like that one. Now, Ivan, I will telephone you from Caracas to tell you what plane you must meet in Jacksonville. Don't forget to take photographs. And behave as you should."

He shook hands with everyone, including Ivan, and got back in his taxi.

Matt had loaded the car with all kinds of odds and ends as well as Alyosha in his box, the picnic hamper and suitcases and a box of Miss Manderby's books— she must, thought Ivan, have worried there might not be any books in Florida. They got into the car. Harry cried "Bon Voyage" and kissed the fender of the car. Then, with a great rattle, Matt started the engine and they were off.

V

"Because we are different," replied Matt. "Distinguished," suggested Miss Manderby. Alyosha, released from his box, was sitting on the top of the front seat just behind Matt's shoulder. Daisies, a parting gift from Harry, drooped in the sunlight from the little vases, and Miss Manderby's picnic basket, its brown straw cracked and curling, took up a whole seat by itself like an extra person. She had, with Matt's permission, lined up a few books on various little ledges around the back seat.

Matt was wearing a black cowboy hat that might have been a size or so too large for him.

Ivan had noticed that during the afternoon the drivers and passengers of other cars frequently turned to stare at them. Sometimes people smiled, occasionally they looked puzzled, and one man had scowled and shaken his head. A small boy, staring at them from the back of a passing station wagon, had made a gun out of his fist and shot them all, even Alyosha. Ivan counted four bangs that the small boy's mouth formed clearly.

"For some people, we are only a moving target," said Miss Manderby.

"Barely moving," added Matt.

"I had thought we could eat an early supper in a meadow by a pond," said Miss Manderby.

If that was what Miss Manderby hoped for, it was unlikely they would ever eat supper, thought Ivan. For hours the highway they had been following wound through an area that did not look like the country at all but like the fragments of a monstrous factory yet to be assembled.

Pipes thrust up out of the ground and curled around themselves. Towers and furnaces rose straight up and dwindled away to vents from which orange flames shot forth. Tanks and spheres as big as apartment houses sat on ground out of which nothing grew. Ivan had not seen one single person moving among all the towers and spheres and furnaces and pipes, and he wondered who took care of them, what they were for and what had existed before they came.

"Sulphur!" Miss Manderby exclaimed at one point, sniffing the air.

"And fire," said Matt.

"The Underworld," said Miss Manderby. "You've taken a wrong turn, Matt."

Matt laughed, and Ivan asked, "What is the Underworld?"

"Hades," said Miss Manderby.

"Hell," said Matt.

They passed the last great sphere, which had been painted a soft eerie blue, and there before them was a meadow. But when they stopped, they discovered signs on trees and fences that read NO TRESPASSING and VIOLATORS WILL BE PROSECUTED.

The signs continued for miles, and finally Matt turned off the highway onto a narrow road full of holes. They continued on this until they came to a field that was not fenced in. There was no pond, but at least there was a little ditch with a trickle of water flowing over and around the tin cans and pop bottles.

Alyosha jumped into the tall grass at once, and all they could see of him as they spread out the table cloth for the picnic was his tail as he followed a path of his own design.

"Grasshoppers, imaginary or otherwise, remarked Miss Manderby. It was getting chilly although the sun still shone, and long shadows lay across the meadow from the row of trees that stood on a slope at the western edge. After they had eaten, Matt and Miss Manderby talked about how far they would drive that night.

"We should be in South Carolina by tomorrow evening," Matt said, and Ivan wandered off, full of roast beef and apple strudel, glad they had escaped from Hades, feeling years away from home and the kitchen table and his school books. A faint breeze sprang up, and as the tawny grass bent and rose beneath it, the meadow seemed to roll around him like a sea tide. Alyosha leaped in front, but sometimes the little cat coiled around his ankles like a snake.

Up toward the slope Ivan saw a gleam of metal and found the wreck of a car half-buried in the grass and earth. The tires were gone as well as the steering wheel, the windows were smashed, and spider webs of glass hung from the window frames. When Matt and Miss Manderby came up to look at it, Ivan asked how had it gotten there. There was no road leading into the field, and no car tracks anywhere.

"Look," said Matt. "There's an old bird's nest on

the back seat. The car has been here a long time."

Alyosha leaped on the roof as Matt reached in through the back window and drew out the empty nest, placing it in Ivan's hand. A few birds flew swiftly across the field as though to get home before dark, and the westering sun stained the sky yellow and green and purple. The three travelers seemed to be the only people left in the world. For a second, as he listened to the silence broken only by the nearly inaudible breath of the wind, the cry of a bird, Ivan was frightened.

"It's the hour of the twilight ghosts," said Miss Manderby.

"There aren't ghosts," said Ivan.

"There could be," said Miss Manderby.

Matt put his cowboy hat on Ivan's head and said, "Let's go collect things. We've got a long way to go."

"Are you ready?" Ivan nodded, feeling all right again.

He woke when they stopped for gas, then fell back to sleep, and once again wakened to bright lights that made the dark blacker. This time he saw a little wooden house with a sign tacked across it reading CABINS BY THE NIGHT, THE WEEK.

An old man with a flashlight in one trembling hand showed them to two cabins beneath some pine trees. Miss Manderby said goodnight and went to her cabin, carrying Alyosha under one arm and a book under the other. There was one room in Matt's cabin, and a bathroom so small that Matt had to go into it sideways. Ivan crawled beneath the slightly damp sheets of his bed. The last thing he saw was the bird's nest on the bedside table, his first souvenir of the trip.

They started out so early the next morning that mist was still rising from the ground. Farms sat off in fields, little frame houses with sagging porches, looking deserted. Yet green things were growing in the fields. They passed beneath trees with blossoms the color of grape jelly, and drove over streams on which the mist rested like a coverlet.

Suddenly Ivan grew aware that the weather had really changed. They had met early spring, and now they were traveling through late spring toward summer.

"We are traveling through time," announced Miss Manderby.

Ivan had two fried egg sandwiches for lunch at a roadside stand where the man who served them spoke English in a soft unfamiliar accent, his voice full of sighs. In the afternoon they passed more farms. Old rusty cars were often piled up in front of them, and sometimes there was a truck, and a man getting down from it and turning his head to look at Harry's car as they drove past.

There weren't many cars on the road, and people no longer looked at them as though they were a curiosity. In the late afternoon they drove through a town where the houses were pink and white, where shutters hid windows, and flowering vines crept along the walls. It was very hot.

Ivan found the trip boring at times. The car seat made him itchy, and it seemed terribly crowded. There was the cat and the big black cowboy hat and the boxes and the books and all Matt's painting equipment and their suitcases. And there was the picnic basket, an apparently endless source of cookies and fruit. But Miss Manderby played geography with him, a game he was quite good at as a result of having looked at maps for so many years instead of reading the information that went with them. She beat him anyhow, downing him at last with Xochimilco, a word he decided he couldn't have spelled if his life depended on it.

When the game grew dull, Miss Manderby produced a very small deck of cards and taught him several kinds of solitaire. She gave him a large book to use for a table. When he got tired of that, Miss Manderby read aloud. It was a story called The Happy Prince.

When she had finished it, he started to ask some questions. Why hadn't the swallow realized it was going to be so cold that he would die? And why, if the Prince could talk to the swallow, didn't he tell the people to leave his gold leaf and his eyes alone?

Then, in the warm car, silent except for Alyosha's purring, Ivan decided the questions were foolish. No one expected him to ask them, and he didn't have to bother. There weren't any answers anyway. After a while Matt sang some songs, a few of which Ivan knew. And so the day passed, and by nightfall they were in South Carolina.

That night they stayed in a motel managed by a lady whose hair was rolled around pink curlers. She bustled around them and fussed and fumed and waved her hands. "You all sure you got everything you want? Isn't the little fellow hungry? How about a little fried-egg sandwich?"

In the morning they started the last lap of the trip. Alyosha seemed livelier, and by now Ivan felt he could have driven another week without minding. The car had become a little house. Miss Manderby bought a straw basket at a roadside store, and Matt bought some old green bottles and a jar of honey that Ivan held upside down to watch the golden bubbles slowly rising.

"Jacksonville!" announced Matt sometime during the late afternoon. Before them, in the heat haze, was a city with tall buildings and bridges and billboards and people and cars.

A little while later, Matt said, "South Jacksonville." And when he pulled the car to the side of the road and took out the map Mr. Crown had sent him, Miss Manderby said, "And this must be East Jacksonville."

"No, it's Amblerville," said Matt.

"But there's nothing here," observed Ivan, looking at a dense forest of thick trees on their left.

"We take that road," said Matt. Ivan saw a narrow sand road leading into the midst of the forest. The car rumbled down a slight incline, and then they were among the trees and the sunlight was lost except for a startling burst of light here or there. The branches of the trees were hung with a lacy tangle of something Matt called Spanish moss. Soon the road split off into other little narrow roads, and Matt had to stop to consult the map.

The trees began to thin. At last they came to a

clearing at the top of a long slope that inclined toward the banks of a great wide river. And between the river and the last line of trees stood an immense house with darkened windows. As they drove around to the front, they saw the beginning of a wide porch from which columns arose to support a triangular roof. The paint was scaling off; there was a yellow tinge to the wood, and a thick twining vine threw its purple-blossomed tendrils across the walls. A broken rocking chair leaned up against a column.

"Look at that!" Matt exclaimed, and he whistled. "Is it real?"

"Almost," said Miss Manderby in a whisper. "But it's fading fast."

At that moment two tall elderly people, a man and a woman, walked out through the double doors. Behind them was a girl with ragged curling hair. She was as tall as Ivan.

"Well, Mr. Mustazza," cried Mr. Crown. "Glad you made it. This is Mrs. Crown, and we are delighted to see all of you." He looked back at the house. "I fear the bulldozers are not far behind you."

"Hello," said the young girl.

"This is our neighbor, Geneva," said Mrs. Crown.

Ivan saw that Geneva was barefooted.

VI

ON THE BROAD SILL OF AN UNFINISHED WINDOW, Alyosha sat blinking in the pale early morning sunshine. Beyond the little cat Ivan could see the limb of a tree, and beyond that was a streak of bright blue glittering like mica, and then three dark gray smudges which, as Ivan sat up in his bed, grew more distinct and became three great gray ships tied up at the city's wharves across the river. An oblong of sunlight lay across the wall above the fireplace. The yellow and red flowers of the wallpaper were almost white. That particular oblong of light must have fallen in that exact spot for so many years it had finally drowned all color, thought Ivan. Where the sunlight could not reach, in the far corners of the room, the paper roses were still bright.

Ivan had been too tired and sleepy the night before

to pay much attention to his room. Now he wandered about it, studying the massive desk with its dozens of small compartments, touching the carved posts of the bed, opening the doors of a huge cupboard and finding inside it nothing but dust and a few papers, their edges curled, the writing faded. There were large holes in the rug on which he walked, and the fantastic birds of the rug's pattern had faded to the colors of their palest feathers.

Alyosha jumped lightly to the floor and padded out of the room, not giving Ivan a passing glance. The house was silent, cool. It must be very early. He went over to the window. Below, the uncut grass looked smoky and damp. To the left and right of the house were thick woods, and straight ahead was the river. Leading out from the bank was a narrow ramshackle dock. The whole construction leaned to one side as though something were pushing it slowly and steadily down to the water.

Carrying his clothes, Ivan went out into the hall, along which were many closed doors twice his height. A circular staircase wound down to the entrance hall below.

After opening several closet doors, Ivan at last found a bathroom. It was as large as his bedroom at home. Except for a small black stove in one corner, everything appeared to be made of marble. When he turned on the tap, only a slight trickle of water dripped onto the cracked marble of the sink. The toilet itself had the most curious arrangement he had ever seen. A long metal chain, with a handle like a jump rope's, hung from a rectangular tank way up near the ceiling. When Ivan pulled the chain there was a noise like barrels being rolled down a ramp, then a great slosh of water. He ran out into the hall. But doors remained closed. No one rushed out to shout "Man the lifeboats!"

The kitchen, a damp cool chamber, was in the back of the house. Here there were two stoves; one was massive, black and smelled of wet cinders. The other was small, dented and electric. In a large bowl on a wooden table in the center of the room he found an orange. Then he took a slice of bread from a package in a cupboard and went out the front doors to the porch. He stood there a while, eating the orange and feeling the empty, cool brightness of the morning. He finished the orange, stuffed the peel into his pocket and walked down the sagging porch steps and onto the grass. A small young dog suddenly emerged from the woods at the right. With its nose to the ground and its four legs propelling it across the lawn, it ran straight into the woods on the left.

The dock was even more dilapidated than it had appeared from his bedroom window. A few planks had been slung between rotted pilings. He scrambled down the incline. Here the slope was a gentle one, but beyond the Crown dock, the banks rose sharply. The river was so wide that Ivan guessed it would take at least an hour to row across it. He breathed in a great gulp of air. It tasted fresh and faintly bitter and watery. Not far from the shore floated large patches of some water plant, and among the green leaves were tightly curled purple blossoms.

It surprised him that there should be a river here, that he should wake up and walk out of a house and come to its banks. The surprise of the river had been in his mind when he observed the little dog, when he walked down the slope, and he was still surprised as he tried to estimate if the dock were strong enough to walk on. It was as though the river were flowing through his mind.

He took an uncertain step onto a plank. Instantly there was a thick shuffling sound, like a laundry bag full of shoes being dragged across the floor. Then he saw three forms at once, and each form was a large gray snake that shot into the water and disappeared into one of the patches of water plant.

Ivan knew little about snakes, but he knew he didn't care for them. If he hadn't been standing there by himself, he might have shouted or run away. But there was no one to shout at or run to, so he stood there and shuddered. The snakes had not looked at all like the baby boa constrictor a boy had brought to school one day in a box that had once held two pounds of chocolates. He had been obliged to pet that snake in order not to seem different, or scared. But he did not think that the three snakes that had slid into the water, like knives into butter, would allow themselves to be petted.

"Water moccasins," said a low voice.

Ivan jumped back from the plank. Geneva was there, a few yards away, sitting in the middle of a small green boat, her hands resting lightly on an oar. He wondered how long she had been there, and how she had managed to be so quiet and whether she had seen him shudder.

"Poisonous," she said. "You always have to kick the dock before you step on it. They like to loop around the pilings and catch the sun." She lifted the oar and poked an island of green plant near the boat.

"They also like to hide out in the hyacinth," she said. "But they don't bother you when you swim."

Ivan had a quick picture of himself, taking a flying jump off the end of the dock into the dark water. He didn't believe he'd ever do it.

"Would you like to take a ride?" she asked.

"Yes," said Ivan.

Geneva brought the little boat around to the shore with great ease. As Ivan stepped into it, he saw, scattered about the planking, a rusty anchor, several coils of rope, some string, an oil can, a fishing pole with a few rusty hooks stuck into the bamboo, a shovel, a paper bag, a small pail, and at the stern, a very dirty motor.

"Why, you've got an outboard motor," he said.

"Well, it works some days," she said. "You sit right there, and I'll get us out of here and onto the river."

With the same ease she had shown before, Geneva rowed the boat out to the open water. "I knew you were coming," she said. "Mr. Crown told us he was going to get a painter down here to make pictures of his house. Then the painter telephoned and asked if he could bring you and that old lady with him, and Mr. Crown said yes."

It had all seemed so easy—Matt asking Ivan,

Ivan's father agreeing. He had no idea people had been speaking about him before he even knew they existed.

"Where do you live?" he asked.

"You'll be able to see my house in a minute," she said, poking at a patch of hyacinth with an oar. And in a minute he saw, up on a steep bank, an old yellow frame house with a porch running all around it. There was the remains of an old dock there, a few pilings, a collapsed plank.

"It looks like the woods are creeping right up to the house," said Geneva, "but there's a little garden in the back with paths and flower beds. The house is so damp the piano won't stay in tune for more than a day. You're lucky you came down at this time of year. Later on it rains every afternoon. My shoes are soaking wet every morning and I have to put them on to go to school. And there are lots of bugs. I don't mind snakes, but I hate bugs."

"What's the name of this river?"

"St. John's," she said. "Later we'll go out and try to catch some swells."

She kneeled over the motor and pushed back her hair. Then she wound a string around something that looked like a gear.

"What are the swells?" Ivan asked, wondering uneasily if she was speaking of whirlpools.

"See those big ships tied up over there at Jacksonville? When they pull out I get as close as I can to them. Then I get a good ride from their wake. Sometimes the sailors yell at me to go away, but I pretend I can't hear them. I keep an eye on them from a little room at the top of my house. As soon as I see they're getting ready to sail, I get the boat. The only trouble is that sometimes the motor won't work and that drives me crazy!"

"Do you go fishing?"

"No," she said. "That's my father's fishing rod. I can't take the hooks out of the fish. My father's gone off to Baton Rouge. There's a Ford assembly plant there, and he went to get a job. Maybe we'll go later on, my mother and me. But I hate to leave the river. I live with my aunt now because my mother's gone to Chattahoochie to take care of my grandmother who's sick. She's a million years old and probably dead by now anyway. Here we go!"

She gave the string a violent yank. The motor coughed and died. She began winding up the string again.

"I've got a friend, Amos L. Adams, who invented

a new kind of flower," she said. "He lives over in Mandarin, on a little bitty river. That painter ought to paint his house. It's much prettier than Mr. Crown's and not all falling apart. Did you know that my house will be exactly twenty-eight yards from the fourteenth hole when they finish that golf course? We may sell the house, except nobody will probably want to buy it for fear of flying golf balk. That's why we want to sell it. They are going to tear up this whole place—trees, ground, rocks, houses, Mr. Crown's house."

"Who is they?" Ivan asked as she gave the string another yank. This time the motor caught, and they putt-putted straight toward the ships.

"They?" she repeated. "I've never been able to find out who they are. But they're always up to something."

Looking back at the shore, Ivan saw Mr. Crown's plantation house. From the river it looked more like a photograph. The trees seemed to have moved in closer, and it had a deserted look.

"How long is your vacation?" Geneva was asking him.

"Until a week from Monday," he said.

"That's what we get," she said. "Lucky we have the same vacation. Mr. Crown didn't want to sell his house.

He loves it, but the roof is full of holes. And he says the only people who'd have money enough to fix it up would just as soon burn it—or build a golf course."

"What kind of flower did you friend invent? How can anyone invent a flower?"

"Well, not invent, I guess. But he combined two different kinds and got a third that was different from the other two. Maybe it was some kind of orchid. They wrote it up in the Florida agricultural record though, and he's only a year or so older than me. I'm twelve."

Here I am, thought Ivan to himself, sitting in the middle of the St. John's river in a green boat, listening to a talking machine named Geneva. He laughed.

"What's funny?" she asked.

"Nothing. I like being in this boat."

She opened the paper bag, her left hand on the tiller.

"Do you like cornbread and raspberry jam?" she asked. "I made myself a little breakfast, but I'd be pleased if you'd have half. Exactly half."

He took out the two pieces of yellow bread stuck together with globs of sweet-smelling jam. "If you divide, I'll choose," said Geneva. "If I divide, you can choose. That way it's fair."

"I'll divide," he said, not wanting her to let go of the tiller.

The cornbread was deliciously gritty and sweet and filling.

"There's oranges too. I thought you might be up, so I brought two of those."

As they drew closer the ships looked larger and more menacing. Ivan could see the great booms swinging back between deck and wharf, anchors as big as the boat they were in, chains of metal links as thick as his arm and cables and wires and ropes, taut or loose, swinging or coiled, but peculiarly animated as though they were living things. At the stern of one of the ships, his foot on the railing, stood a man in a peaked blue cap, staring intently across the river.

"That's a freighter," said Geneva, shutting off the motor. When the sound died, Ivan felt a stab of fear. The water must be so deep. It was so black. They were so far from the other shore.

He hadn't told Geneva that this was the first time he'd ever been on a river, and that he'd never even been in a boat. He had had swimming lessons, but that only meant he could swim in a pool. If you put a pool in a river, it would disappear, he thought.

"You can tell it's a freighter," Geneva was

explaining, "because the quarters are in the center. My father told me that. He used to be a seaman and shipped out until he married my mother. Now he has a hard time finding a job. Let's have the oranges."

They looked at the ships and ate their oranges. "You can throw the peel over," she said. "It just sinks. Look, there's something coming."

Ivan threw the peel overboard, then emptied his pocket of the old peel somewhat secretly, not wanting her to know, for some reason, that he'd already had an orange. He followed the direction of her pointing finger and saw a trim little tugboat coming toward them at considerable speed. Geneva bent to the motor, and this time it fired at once. She took them out of the path of the oncoming boat. After it had passed them on the starboard side, she cut the motor, smiled at Ivan and held up a finger. "Now, watch!" she whispered.

In less than a minute the little green boat started to rock gently. Suddenly it swooped, its nose heading right into a large wave. Back and forth it swung, up the wave, down the other side. Geneva laughed and hung onto the gunnels. They were sprayed with water, and Ivan shut his eyes. Then the boat was still.

"See?" she asked. "Those are swells."

After that she took him back to the Crown dock, promising she would come back for him in the afternoon. "I'll take you up one of the creeks if those freighters are still docked," she said. The boat slid up on the muddy shore.

"Lots of snakes now," she observed. Ivan looked at the dock. There must have been six or seven moccasins hanging from the pilings and planks like spare tires.

"Have you got snakes like that up your way?" she asked.

It was the first question she'd asked him about where he'd come from. He told her about the boa constrictor in full detail, feeling he owed her a long story. She kept one foot over the side of the boat, on the ground, and the boat slid slightly with the small movement of the water against the shore. She looked surprised and interested.

"We couldn't bring a snake to school here," she said. "The blue racers aren't poisonous, but you couldn't get them to stay in a box."

"Thanks for the cornbread," Ivan said.

"Okay," she said, and pushed off with her foot and began to row her way along the shore toward home.

PAULA FOX

VII

IVAN DISCOVERED MATT ON THE LAWN, A SKETCHbook in his hand. Matt waved. "Morning." "I've been all the way across the river," Ivan said. "I saw you in the boat," Matt replied.

Miss Manderby, a green scarf around her head, had propped up the broken rocking chair against the wall and was sitting there smiling at Ivan, an open book in her lap.

"Look at the wisteria," she said. "Smell the air! Mrs. Crown has thousands of books, and she has asked me to help her sort them out. Some she intends to keep, but the rest will go to the library. We are going to begin the work after lunch. I think I have died and gone to heaven."

"I've been across the river," said Ivan.

"Mr. Crown told us Geneva would be around to

fetch you," said Miss Manderby.

"Where is Baton Rouge, Chattahoochie and Mandarin?" Ivan asked.

"Baton Rouge is in Louisiana," said Miss Manderby. "As for the other places, I've found a splendid map of the United States in the drawing room. We'll go see. I think Chattahoochie—what an extraordinary name—is in Florida."

Ivan and Miss Manderby went into the drawing room, a darkened cavern in which massive carved overstuffed furniture sat in the gloom like monstrous toads. Long red dusty curtains covered the windows, and on the walls were portraits of people wearing wardrobes of clothes with stiff dry-looking faces and eyes that seemed to follow a person about the room. Miss Manderby found Chattahoochie and Mandarin in Florida, the latter being only a few miles away from Amblerville.

She went back to her book, and Ivan wandered about the Crown house finding rooms empty of furniture, and the dust on the floor so thick he could draw pictures in it with his finger. He thought about Geneva who was certainly unusual. The girls in his class, most of them anyhow, already seemed grown up in certain unpleasant ways. They laughed a lot in high unreal voices, and when the teacher asked them to form a line with the boys to go to lunch or to the library, they made terrible faces and screamed disgust sounds until they were quieted down.

After lunch Ivan went to wait for Geneva on the dock, kicking it first to make the snakes fly off. He was glad to see her when she came rowing toward him, and they set off up the river. Those ships were parked, she said, so they might as well go to a creek. There were quite a few small streams leading into the river, but only one or two were wide and deep enough to be navigable.

Going up the creek was like breaking into the middle of a jungle movie, Ivan thought. Long vines hung from the thick limbs of trees, the tree trunks hidden by the thick bright underbrush. The little stream shimmered and broke into ripples, which abruptly flattened out into mysterious pools where Ivan spotted the dark shapes of fish. There were sweet-smelling flowers hanging from some of the trees, and although the sun was very hot, it was cool beneath the Spanish moss and vines and flowers.

"I've brought you my book," said Geneva. Ivan's heart sank. Another reader!

But it was only a scrapbook she put in his hand.

"I'm going to draw all the things in the world," she said, and hooked the anchor behind a rock on the creek bank. "Now, look inside."

He opened to the first page and found dozens of drawings, some so tiny he had to squint to see them. There was a fork, a toad, a leaf, a gull, a frying pan, a pin, an orange, a lady's shoe, the wheel of a car, a sink with two taps, a twig, a doorknob, a bottle, a cup, a snake, a hammer, an oar, a necklace of beads, a palm leaf, an ant.

"There's a lot more," she said, and he turned the page. Here were a pair of glasses, and on the other side of one of the lenses, a grasshopper. Then there was a front door, a bench, a little heap of round stones, a stethoscope, a dollar bill, a dog, a book, a pocketknife, a cereal bowl. He looked through the rest of the book. It must have taken her months to draw all those things, he thought. When he had finished, Geneva, who had been sitting quietly in the bow, said, "Now look at the cover."

He turned over the scrapbook. On it, in large green letters, was written: The Book of Things. Volume One. Seen and Drawn by Geneva Colrain.

"What do you think?" she asked.

"It's wonderful," he said. That was not a word he

could remember using before, and although he had heard it once or twice, it felt unfamiliar. Then he told her about his mother and grandmother and uncle leaving Russia and crossing the border and going to Warsaw, and how Matt was drawing a picture of them crossing that border in a sledge.

"I'd like to see that," she said.

"I don't know whether he brought it or not."

"Let's go back and find out," she said, and dropped the anchor back in the boat, and they went downstream to the river and back to the Crown dock.

Everyone was sitting on the porch drinking lemonade. Mrs. Crown, who must have been quite absentminded, poured lemonade for Ivan and Geneva onto the tray. Perhaps it was because she was holding an animated conversation with Miss Manderby about someone named Emerson. In any case, she simply smiled when she saw what she had done, and poured two full glasses.

Matt had brought the drawing, and he took Ivan and Geneva to his room on the first floor behind the kitchen. Ivan smiled when he saw the room because Matt had made it look like his studio back home. He'd pushed all the furniture into a corner except for one long table in the middle of the room that he had covered with newspapers. On it were all of Matt's things—his palette knives and pencils and brushes and paint and sketch pads. He lifted all the pads and took out the drawing of the sledge.

Geneva looked at the sledge, the sentries, the horses, the driver, the pines and the sentry box for a long time.

"You haven't got the people in it yet," she said at last.

"Not yet," said Matt. "But they'll be along."

"Show him The Book of Things," Ivan said to Geneva.

She handed the scrapbook to Matt. He took it over to the window and opened it. Ivan liked Matt for taking Geneva's work over to the window where he could get the best light. He couldn't say exactly why he liked it; it was just the way Matt was.

Matt looked carefully at each page, and when he had finished the book, he said to Geneva, "I like everything you've put down, especially the grasshopper behind the eyeglasses. The snake is very good. You might try drawing it in other ways besides being coiled up. Half-coiled, or hanging from a tree, or with its head resting on a twig. The more ways you draw it, the more you will understand what a snake is." He handed her back the scrap book, then gave her two pieces of charcoal. "You might try using these too. If they break, don't give it a thought. Use even the smallest bits."

Later, Geneva and Ivan got into the boat and rowed down to her dock. His oar kept slipping out of his hand, but all she said was, "You'll catch on, after a while." Then she told him there was a path through the woods between the Crown and Colrain houses. "I'll show it to you sometime. It's faster than the boat but not as good."

The grass was tall right up to the porch steps at Geneva's house. After the Crown place, it was like going from a big railroad station to a little country depot. The hall was only a few steps long, and the stairs took up most of the space. There was a smell of dampness in the air, and old furniture and wood-wax. Geneva's room was bare. The walls were white-washed, and there was a single light cord and bulb hanging from the center of the ceiling. Dampness had drawn random designs on the plaster. Near a door that led to the porch, a pair of brown thick-soled shoes lay on their sides.

"For school," she said, when she saw he was looking at them. "No good for the boat."

A small table held a few school books, and lying open was another scrapbook. "Volume Two," said Geneva when he went to see what she had drawn. The only object on the page was a bathtub with large feet shaped like animal claws.

"Our bathtub," she said. "This section will have everything in the bathroom, even the toothbrushes and little bits of soap my aunt saves.

In the kitchen, Miss Weller, Geneva's aunt, was stirring something in a pot.

"Brush your hair, Geneva," she said in a tone of voice that Ivan knew meant she had said it a thousand times before. "You're Ivan. You look just the way Geneva described you. She describes very well. You'd think for such a talker she'd be able to write good descriptions for her English teacher. But she doesn't. She forgets punctuation and gets jam all over the paper. Perhaps if you'd brush your hair, Genny, you'd be able to write better."

"Can we have some chocolate cookies?" asked Geneva.

After they went into the little garden behind the house, Geneva said, "If you ask them for something, they forget what they were telling you to do. Or if you don't say anything at all, they get confused. That's the good thing about them—they're so forgetful."

Geneva's hair looked like yellow Spanish moss.

She showed him the piano that was permanently out of tune, and they both hit a few notes to see just how sour they would sound. Then they went down to the wharf. There was only one plank still nailed on. The rest were rotting in the shallow water.

"I swim off the Crown's dock because we never get around to fixing this," she said. She looked up at the sky. "My father taught me how to predict the weather. And I predict it's going to rain any minute." To Ivan, the sky looked as sunny and blue as it had in the morning.

But a short time later, as they walked the narrow path through the woods, Ivan heard the raindrops hitting the leaves, although the trees were so thick he didn't feel a drop. The woods were silent except for their footfalls. Geneva told him that once she had managed to get from one end of the path to the other with only one noise, and that had been when she screeched because a racer had dropped from a branch to her feet.

"It was the surprise," she said. "I'm pretty used to snakes." She had been trying to get down that path for a year and not make a single sound—"like a ghost," she explained—but something always happened. After he heard that, Ivan walked stiffly, keeping an eye on the long thick branches of the trees in case a racer, or anything else, looked like it might fall down his shirt. When they emerged on the Crown lawn, the rain was falling steadily.

"I'll get Amos L. Adams over here tomorrow so he can explain to you about that flower," she said.

That evening, Matt took Ivan off to a movie in South Jacksonville, and afterward they went to a place where they had two hamburgers each and a bowl of tough, chewy French fries, and then they played the pinball machine for an hour or two. When they got back to the house, the windows were dark, and only a frail light shone from the hall.

The sky had cleared, and a full moon hung just above the river, its light streaking the water with a mysterious glitter. The house looked haunted, but not by ghosts. Ivan felt as if they had walked into a private place where things were happening that had nothing to do with him and Matt, nothing to do with anyone at all. The night air, the silver streak of moon-light and the faint sound of water lapping the shore seemed to make one simple but unknown sound, as though some very large and unimaginable creature were breathing quietly to itself in the night.

Early the next morning Ivan found Geneva waiting for him in her green boat, and they went off to catch the swells. They had luck because one of the big freighters was leaving the wharf to begin its journey down the river to the ocean.

The little boat dipped down into a huge trough left by the wake of the ship, then slid violently up on the other side, down again and up. Ivan and Geneva held onto the gunnels, shrieking and laughing, their feet banging against the bottom of the boat. When the waves had subsided, Ivan found himself soaked through and through.

That afternoon he set off on the path to Geneva's house. He walked so woodenly that he felt as if someone had slipped a coat hanger into his shirt and, at any minute, was going to hang him up on a closet clothing bar. In front of Geneva's house he found a car very much like Harry's, except this one was dusty and didn't have flower vases.

The car belonged to Amos L. Adams, as he soon discovered, and Ivan was astonished that a boy not much older than he would actually be allowed to drive a car. Looking at that car, thinking about his life in the city, Ivan realized that he was nearly always being taken to or from some place by an adult, that in nearly every moment of his day he was holding onto a rope held at the other end by a grown-up person—a teacher or a bus driver, a housekeeper or a relative. But since he had met Matt, space had been growing all around him. It was frightening to let go of that rope, but it made him feel light and quick instead of heavy and slow.

Amos L. Adams, who came out of Geneva's house a moment later carrying an enormous lily in a clay pot, was wearing a white shirt with the sleeves rolled up. He was tall and thin, and when he smiled, which was often, he looked like a clown. He didn't know where to put the lily, which he had brought for Geneva, and finally she told him just to set it down any old place. Then the three of them sat on the porch steps. Amos never did explain about his special invented flower, but spoke instead of his dogs and the various tricks he had taught them.

"Amos knows a lot," said Geneva at some point in the conversation, and Ivan felt envious. No one, he thought, was likely to say that he knew a lot.

"About some things," Amos added modestly.

Miss Weller promised that if they'd go to the garden, she'd bring them a pitcher of iced tea. They stayed there an hour or so, drinking the cold amber tea, talking about dogs and snakes. Amos explained that the reason you could never really make a snake friendly was because snakes were hatched from eggs. They took care of themselves right from the beginning, and had nothing to do with their snake parents.

"All they can do is lie around looking pretty or ugly. But dogs have regular mamas, so you can make a friend out of a dog."

Ivan thought about that for some time. It worried him. He wondered if there was some vague similarity between himself and a snake. At the same time, he knew it was ridiculous to think of himself in such a way. After all, there were people who had taken care of him. Besides, he was friendly.

In the latter part of the afternoon, Amos drove them to his house in Mandarin to show them his dogs. They had to stop for some time on the road while Amos pulled a long snake out of the way. It had been stretched right across the road, asleep.

"Must have eaten something," said Geneva.

Ivan abandoned the idea that he had anything in common with snakes except that he and they both lived on the earth, and breathed.

Amos' house was prettier than the Crown house but not as interesting. It was brand new, and it sat only a few yards from a little river. A line of trees on the bank drooped their branches right into the water. As they sat on the bank, Amos' dogs, sleek and black and playful, swarmed all over them. Amos had his own garden where he grew his experimental flowers, and his room was full of books and of plants in pots.

Ivan looked through Amos' microscope. At first he saw nothing, then Amos put something on a piece of glass and slid it under the eyepiece. Ivan saw a great moist-looking luminous bubble, inside of which were valleys and ridges and floating things. When he looked away from the microscope to see what Amos had put beneath it, he saw a green leaf with a drop of water on it. He wondered how it would be to see everything under a microscope. If he had microscopic eyes, he'd never be able to agree with anyone.

When he got home that afternoon, he looked at Alyosha who was lying on the porch, switching his tail. Did the cat see him as he saw himself? He bent forward to look closely at Alyosha's eyes. They were peculiar, like little moons of jello. Alyosha suddenly leaped into the air and skittered away sideways. Miss Manderby, emerging from the house at that second, said, "You must have been staring at him. He does that when he's stared at. I have the same impulse myself under such conditions, but not the means to carry it out."

He smiled at Miss Manderby. He didn't understand half of what she said, but it didn't seem to matter. His father's sentences were so short, Ivan could actually count the number of words in them. Yet he always felt a flock of questions after his father spoke to him. "I'm off to Chicago," his father would say. Ivan would fidget and tell himself that what his father had said was perfectly clear.

But somehow, he didn't understand what his father was telling him. Of course, he knew what the words meant—they meant his father would board an airplane at one airport, and get off the plane at another. But what on earth did that mean?

He told Miss Manderby about Amos and his house down by the river.

"Did you notice any books lying around?" asked Miss Manderby.

"He had a lot in his room—books about plants and dogs, things like that."

"Well, then, he'll be all right," said Miss Manderby vaguely, dusting off her skirt. "I must get back to my work. We've found three sets of the works of Sir Walter Scott. Imagine!"

Ivan found Matt in his room. The painter was looking through the day's sketches he had made, putting one or two aside, stuffing the rest into a paper sack.

"I was just thinking about you," said Matt. "I was thinking it must be terrific to go out in Geneva's boat."

"It is," said Ivan.

"I'm about to add something to the sledge," said Matt. He got out the drawing and spread it on the table, then picked up the black crayon. He stared down at the paper.

"It's strange to work outdoors the way I've been doing," he said. "Painters used to work from nature, but now all that is changed."

Matt's hand was hovering directly over the sledge, and Ivan felt a little cramp of fear—perhaps it was excitement. Then Matt began to draw.

"It's Miss Manderby!" exclaimed Ivan. And it certainly was, although this Miss Manderby was not wearing a scarf but a thick fur hood that covered her hair. She was huddled in a corner of the sledge, most of her covered with a furry looking robe, and her intent gaze was bent upon the blank space between herself and the driver.

"I would like to put Alyosha in too," said Matt.

"Do you think they would have taken a cat?"

"They might have taken a cat," said Matt. In a few minutes Ivan saw a little cat curled up on the lap of the lady who was supposed to be his grandmother, but who was really Miss Manderby.

"While I'm at it," Matt said, "I'll add your uncle to this growing crowd." Then he drew a boy about Ivan's age next to the grandmother. The boy looked quite a bit like the painter himself. Oddly enough, the blank white space seemed larger than ever. Ivan felt his mother was already there, cloaked by the paper, waiting to be revealed.

That evening Miss Manderby said he must learn to play bridge so that he could be her partner in a game with Mr. and Mrs. Crown. Bridge was not like chess, which Uncle Gilbert had taught him years before. But he liked it, possibly because he learned quickly. Miss Manderby cautioned him that it took a long time to be really good.

The four of them sat at a rickety table in the drawing room beneath an amber-shaded light that flickered out from time to time, while Matt looked through the Crown family album off in a corner by himself. The long-departed Crowns gazed down at them from their portraits on the wall while everyone played their cards and Miss Manderby wrote down the game score on a scrap of paper.

The Crowns won, but Miss Manderby just smiled when Ivan said he was sorry he hadn't played better. "For me, it's the game, not the winning," she said.

The following morning Geneva announced that that day they must have a swim. They would wait until noon, she said, because then the sun would be at its hottest.

Ivan hardly said a word when he went out with her in the boat, and when he did speak his voice was cranky. He was scared out of his wits at the very thought of jumping off that dock into thousands of snakes. Every other minute he considered just telling her he couldn't do it. But it was not until he met her at the dock in his bathing trunks that he finally said, "Listen. I'm really scared about those moccasins."

Geneva pounded the planks vigorously with her fist, and Ivan heard a series of sinister splashes. Then she came and stood close to him and said, "I've been swimming here since I was three, and the Crowns swim when it gets warmer. Everybody who lives along this riverbank has been swimming all these years, and nobody has been bitten by a moccasin, although my aunt told me that several people have died of pneumonia from staying in the water too long. That may not be true because they tell you things sometimes just to make you behave. But you have to believe someone, and it might just as well be me."

As she spoke, she had been slowly moving away from him and now, at her last word, she raced to the end of the dock and jumped off it. There was a great splash, a shriek and the next thing Ivan saw was Geneva's shining face and mop of hair emerging from the water.

It was a terrible moment for Ivan as, frozen with indecision, he stared at the water, at Geneva shaking herself in it like a happy dog shakes himself after a swim. Then, unexpectedly, Matt said from behind Ivan, "What a great idea! That's what I want, a swim, and I didn't even know it."

As though released from a spell, Ivan moved and flung himself into the river. A few minutes later Matt joined them, and they swam around for a while, then pulled themselves up on the dock to dry off. Ivan felt wonderful, cool to his bones, but he did not think he could ever really get over being scared, and Geneva seemed to read his mind because she said, "You have to be used to it not to worry."

She never asked him to swim with her again, and he was grateful. Every morning they went out in the boat. When there were no ships to make swells for them, they went up the creek again. Once they took a picnic, one of Miss Manderby's specials that she had prepared in the Crown's big damp kitchen. Geneva said it was the best picnic she had ever had in her entire life. And one day, Amos L. Adams came and drove them to an ocean beach. They scrambled through palmettoes and shrubs until they came smack up against towering sand dunes. On the other side was a great long beach, emptied of everything except sea gulls. They slid down the dunes all day, and Amos showed them little creatures that lived in the wet sand, and explained to them how the sharp-bladed sea grass grew in the shifting sand of the dunes, and how the tides ground stones into sand, and how you could tell what kind of stones they were by the color of the sand.

They came home sticky with salt, patchy with sand, to Geneva's kitchen where Miss Weller had just taken four fresh loaves of bread from the oven. She buttered a loaf while Amos and Geneva and Ivan sat at the kitchen table and watched. Then she cut them thick buttery slabs of the hot bread. From a little cabinet with a meshed screen door, she took a large white bowl of freshly made applesauce that smelled of lemon and cinnamon. Then she poured them three large glasses of cold milk.

"My father always calls a good day 'a day at the beach,'" said Geneva.

"Tomorrow is Sunday," said Amos L. "And the next day is Monday."

"School," said Geneva.

Ivan said nothing. He'd run into a wall called Sunday. He'd be going home tomorrow.

When he got back to the Crown house, Miss Manderby had a message for him. "Your father has telephoned from Caracas," she said. "He will be landing at the Jacksonville airport tomorrow. Matt is to drive you there, and then you and your father will take another plane for home. He especially asked me to ask you if you had taken enough photographs."

Ivan's camera lay upside down beneath a pile of soiled shirts in his room. It was full of film, and there were three extra rolls his father had given him for the trip. He had not taken one picture. In fact, he had completely forgotten that the camera was there.

It was still light enough to take a few pictures now. What would his father like? A moccasin hanging from the dock? He picked up the camera, then put it down. He was not going to take any pictures. He would tell his father he'd gotten sand in the lens.

No. He wouldn't do that either. He wouldn't explain. He'd say he hadn't thought about pictures, and that was the truth.

Mrs. Crown had made a party dinner for his last evening, heaps of fried chicken and cornbread pudding and angel food cake. Matt had made a quart of chocolate ice cream before dinner, sitting out on the back steps in the twilight and turning the crank on the ice cream freezer.

When Ivan went to bed that night, he was frightened of the whole house, as though it had turned against him in some way. He lay awake in the dark listening to the wind blowing outside, the creakings and groans and sawlike noises of the house. Then Alyosha stole silently into his room and jumped on the bed to lay next to him, purring softly. So at last he was able to sleep, his hand on one of Alyosha's paws.

Geneva was not waiting for him Sunday morning in her boat. He and Matt had to leave at nine o'clock, and so at eight Ivan walked through the woods to Geneva's house.

She was in the parlor, her hair brushed and combed and held in the back by a peach-colored ribbon. She was wearing a starchy dress and her brown school shoes. As she sat near a window gazing through it at the river, she looked very different.

She glanced up as he walked in. "I have to go to church with my aunt," she said. "That's why I'm dressed up. My father doesn't make me go to church. He says he can take it or leave it. But he's not here now."

Ivan sat down on the piano stool. They were silent for a moment. Then Ivan said, "I have to go now. My father is going to be at the airport, and we're going to fly home."

"I've never been in a plane except a little Piper Cub that I went up in for twenty minutes," she said. "They have a special ride on weekends for people who want to see what it's like."

"What time do you have to go to school in the morning?" he asked.

"I walk out to the road and meet the school bus at 8:05. It's always late though."

"Well, I'll be going," he said.

He stared at her profile for a moment, aware that she had not yet looked right at him. Then he realized all at once that one large transparent tear was slowly moving down Geneva's cheek. It was so startling that

Ivan stood up at once as though someone had shouted his name from a window. Suddenly, she turned to face him. She did not try to brush away that tear, but held out her hand. He shook it and backed out of the room.

"If you ever decide to play golf, maybe you could come down here and try out the new course," she said.

Once he was back on the path in the woods, Ivan recalled Geneva's parlor, and Geneva herself sitting there in her starched dress and brown shoes, as though it were all a distant memory. He had not thought anyone would ever be sorry to see him go. He had not ever thought about that at all.

VIII

GOOD TIME HAD BY ALL? ASKED IVAN'S FATHER AS the plane lifted from the runway.

"Yes," said Ivan. The seat belt made him feel like a prisoner.

"I'll have your pictures developed this afternoon as soon as we get back."

"I didn't take any," Ivan said.

"Didn't take any! Now what's the point of having all that expensive equipment if you don't use it? What's the point of going anywhere if you can't keep a record?"

"I forgot," said Ivan softly. "I forgot until Miss Manderby said you'd called. Then I found the camera under my clothes."

"Someday you may want to see where you've been. Then what will you do?"

"But I know where I was!" exclaimed Ivan.

Portrait *of* Ivan

"I might as well have spared myself the cost of getting you those cameras.

A while later the pilot announced over the public address system that they were flying over North Carolina. Ivan, who had been looking through pictures in a magazine, and finding them boring, said, "But you have no pictures of my mother."

His father did not answer at once. When Ivan looked at him, his father turned away and stared at the passengers across the aisle. Ivan wished it were two minutes earlier, and that he hadn't said those words. His father turned back.

"I do have one picture," he said. "I saved it. It's a marriage picture, taken the day we were married. I'll show it to you, if you want to see it. I sent all the others to your Uncle Vladimir in Paris. I found I was spending all my time looking at them."

Ivan understood what his father had said.

In the afternoon, before he'd unpacked his canvas bag, his father brought Ivan the picture.

It had been taken on a lawn. A breeze must have been blowing, for she was holding down her wide hat, the brim of which curled back around her hand. Ivan looked at it a long time while his father stood silently in the doorway.

PAULA FOX

She did not look at all as Ivan had thought she would. She was thin, with a narrow face and dark hair that curled around her cheeks. She was wearing a suit, and one foot was half lifted from her narrow pointed shoe.

"I like that one," his father said suddenly. "It's because of her shoe. The shoes were new for the wedding, and too tight. She had been standing for a long time, greeting all the wedding guests. When I took that picture, she had gone off by herself. She didn't know that I was there, and she had just lifted her foot from the shoe."

Ivan handed the picture back, and his father took it and said he'd have to go to the office now and "check up on everything."

Later on, Giselle came and made Ivan supper. His father had telephoned to say he would be busy that evening. Ivan was glad to see Giselle. It was nice to sit at the table in his own kitchen, but he was terribly sad, and when he went to bed, he lay awake for a long time. Everything had changed in ten days, changed more than things change in a year. It was as if Ivan had moved to another city, even another country. Everything that should have been familiar was strange.

He guessed he wouldn't see Miss Manderby again. She was staying with the Crowns to help Mrs. Crown with the books and the china and the paintings. And Matt said that after he drove Harry's car back home, he would need only one more sitting. People were staying away, or going away, and nothing was the same.

In school the next day no one asked him where he had been, and he didn't mind because he didn't feel like talking about it. But gradually the day became like other days.

Uncle Gilbert dropped by on Wednesday, and Ivan felt a little better. He told Uncle Gilbert about the snakes and the boat, Geneva and Amos L. Adams, and the river. Then Uncle Gilbert said he'd like to take Ivan to Paris that summer for a trip. He had to go to an international convention of numismatists.

"Of what?" asked Ivan.

"Coin collectors and buyers and sellers," replied Uncle Gilbert. "I thought you'd like to go along to meet your uncle, the other uncle whom you've never seen. He lives in Paris, and I wrote him last month to make sure he'd be there in August. I didn't mention it for fear of disappointing you. But he is going to be there, and he's very happy at the thought of seeing you. You know, you have some cousins too that you've never met. They are older than you."

"I saw a photograph of my mother," said Ivan, fiddling with the wood puzzle his uncle had brought him, hidden inside an apple.

"How did you manage that?" asked Uncle Gilbert.

"I asked my father why he didn't have any pictures, and he said he did have one, and he showed it to me. Do you remember what it was like when you were a baby?"

"It's all cloaked in mystery, my boy," answered Uncle Gilbert. "I may remember, but I can't remember what I remember, if I make myself clear. Your mother was a very nice girl. When your father brought her back here from Paris, after they were married, the first thing she did when she saw me was to hug me. And she could hardly speak a word of English then. Just Russian and French and Italian and a little German."

The puzzle suddenly came apart the way it was supposed to do. Ivan looked at it for a moment, trying to figure out how to put it back together again.

"How did she die?" he asked at last.

His uncle replied instantly as though he'd been waiting for that question.

"She swam away from us," he said. "She loved to swim, and she went too far out, and couldn't get back, and she drowned."

"Where was I?" asked Ivan as he threw down the puzzle.

"On a blanket on the beach, finding out how sand tasted."

"Didn't anyone try to rescue her?"

"We all tried. But we were too late."

Ivan looked at his uncle for a long moment. Then his uncle said, "I know a poem by heart. I'd like to say it to you, Ivan."

"I don't much like poems," said Ivan.

"Just this one ..."

"All right," said Ivan.

Uncle Gilbert cleared his throat and began to recite:

He lay outstretched upon the sunny wave,
That turned and broke into eternity.
The light showed nothing but a glassy grave
Among the trackless tumuli of the sea.
Then over his buried brow and eyes and lips
From every side flocked in the homing ships.

When he had stopped reciting, Ivan said, "That's about a he, not a she. And anyway, I don't know what it means."

"It's about all lost swimmers," said Uncle Gilbert.

A few days later Matt called and asked Ivan to come and sit the following Saturday. When Ivan arrived, the door to the studio was open. Matt was standing in the middle of the room, wearing his cowboy hat and smiling. Ivan ran to him, and Matt hugged him and said, "Good to see you!" Then he showed Ivan all the sketches he had made of the Crown house, and told him about Miss Manderby, and how happy she was to spend a month down there. Geneva had come by every afternoon, after school, just to say hello.

Ivan sat in the old wooden chair. Later they had coffee in the tin mugs, and Matt told Ivan that soon he was going to San Francisco.

"It's cheaper out there for a painter to live," he said. "And the winters are easy."

"And you won't come back here?"

"Oh, I'll come back," Matt said. "I always do."

"My uncle may take me to Paris for a short trip," said Ivan.

"You're lucky," said Matt. "It's good luck to go to Paris."

They went to look at Matt's drawing of the sledge.

"I saw a picture of my mother," Ivan said, looking at the space that was still empty in the sledge. "I remembered her better before I knew what she looked like."

"How old did you tell me she was when they went to Warsaw?" asked Matt.

"About three. But it doesn't matter, I guess." Then it was time to leave, and Matt said they'd see each other again. If he found a good place to live and work, perhaps Ivan could come out and visit him in California. Ivan looked at the studio for the last time. He saw the nail where he'd hung his jacket when it was still cold enough to wear one, and the rocking chair where he'd first seen Miss Manderby, and all of Matt's working things. Then he took a big sniff of linseed oil.

"I'll see you," he said to Matt.

Matt laughed, and said, "Not if I see you first!"

During the last week of school, Ivan's father brought home the portrait of Ivan as well as a large package wrapped in brown paper.

"Mr. Mustazza sent you this," he said, handing Ivan the package. "What do you think of your portrait?"

Ivan looked at it, then at all the photographs of himself in the living room. Then Giselle came in and looked at the portrait.

"That is Ivan," she said.

In the portrait the boy was staring intently out of the painting. The wooden chair was tipped back slightly as though he had pushed against the floor with his feet. He was not smiling. It looked the way Ivan felt.

"It's okay," he said.

He took the package to his room. It was the drawing of the sledge. A note slipped out of the wrappings: "Ivan, I thought the crayon might smudge, so I had this framed for you. I liked doing your portrait and drawing this." It was signed: "Your friend, Matt."

Ivan looked at the little girl in the fur robe who now sat just in front of the older woman and next to the boy. He saw right away that the girl looked quite a lot like Geneva.

He found a hammer and a nail, and he hung the picture on the wall so that he could see it from his bed. After dinner he came back to his room and lay down and looked up at it. The days were getting long now. The room was filled with the soft light of early evening.

Across the snow, the powerful horses pulled the black sledge. The branches of the pine trees were bowed with the weight of snow.

A soldier raced to halt the rearing lead animals, his hand outstretched, his mouth open as though to cry out.

In the sledge huddled the two children who would not see their father again. The little girl did not know she had begun a journey that led right to this room where her son now lay, half asleep. What had she thought, sitting there in the frosty air among the fur robes and the small Oriental rugs?

Then Ivan caught sight of the little cat sitting on the older woman's lap—the woman who was supposed to be his grandmother.

Thinking of Alyosha, Ivan smiled. The sledge had been filled up with people he knew, Harry and Matt, Geneva and Miss Manderby. Somewhere in his mind, an empty ghost sledge raced across the snow. But this one would do for now.

PAULA FOX

PAULA FOX

Paula Fox was born in New York City in 1923 and currently lives in Brooklyn, NY. When she was eight she moved to a Cuban plantation and stayed for two years. Before and after Cuba, she seldom lived anyplace longer than a year or so. She is the author of several books for adults among which are *Desperate Characters: A Novel* and *Borrowed Finery: A Memoir.* Her many books for children include the Newbery Award winning novel, *The Slave Dancer,* and the Newbery Honor Award winning *One-eyed Cat.*